"Do I still make you nervous, Carly?"

Carly's mind flitted back to a dozen years ago, when he'd first asked her that. He'd looked at her with the casual arrogance of an eighteen-year-old male, and asked her how old she was.

"Fourteen. Fifteen in five months."

"And never been kissed I bet."

His challenge made her do something quite out of character. It made her lie. "Yes, I have."

Something in his eyes flared to life, as though she'd unwittingly thrown down the gauntlet. "Well, if that's true then you won't mind if I do this."

Before she even knew what was happening he had swooped down to cover her mouth with his. His lips were a combination of tobacco and hot-blooded male. It was scary and delicious and forbidden.

"I think you have real potential, Miss Carly," he said with a devilish grin. "Look me up anytime you want more."

Then he'd left her breathless. Now... well, maybe he still did, but she'd be damned if she'd spend her summer looking for lost treasure with a man who didn't know right from wrong... or lust from love.

"(Lynn) Lockhart takes us on a wonderful journey as she shows us that the true treasure is love."
—Debbie Richardson, *Romantic Times*

Dear Reader,

You're about to behold a "Rising Star!"
Four of them, to be exact. This month, we're
launching into the galaxy of American Romance a
new constellation—the stars of tomorrow...four
authors brand-new to our series.

And they're just in time to celebrate with us the tenth
anniversary of American Romance. In honor of this
occasion, we've got a slew of surprises in store this
year. "Rising Star" is just the beginning!

Join me, then, and welcome Lynn Lockhart to
American Romance.

Lynn can't pinpoint the exact moment she decided to
be a writer as well as a reader, but once she set her
first words on paper, she never looked back. That
love of books led her to a master's degree in library
science. She now makes her home in a small
Missouri town with her husband, four cats and two
dogs.

Don't wait another minute. Turn the page and catch
a "Rising Star"!

Sincerely,

Debra Matteucci
Senior Editor & Editorial Coordinator
Harlequin
300 East 42nd St.
New York, NY 10017

Lynn Lockhart

DATE WITH AN OUTLAW

Harlequin Books

TORONTO • NEW YORK • LONDON
AMSTERDAM • PARIS • SYDNEY • HAMBURG
STOCKHOLM • ATHENS • TOKYO • MILAN
MADRID • WARSAW • BUDAPEST • AUCKLAND

For my mom, who always believed in me.

For my dad, who taught me that persistence always pays off.

And for my own Missouri Outlaw, who selflessly provided everything I needed to attain my dream.

Published August 1993

ISBN 0-373-16498-X

DATE WITH AN OUTLAW

Printed in U.S.A.

Chapter One

Deke grabbed wildly at the empty air as the sensation of falling gripped him. His hands slammed against metal rails, then closed around them desperately until he realized they were the sides of a bed and that he'd been dreaming. His heartfelt groan of relief echoed off the ceiling, although his pounding heart still seemed capable of beating itself out of his chest.

Gingerly he opened one eye and looked around, then fell back against the skimpy excuse for a mattress with another groan as a shooting pain along the nape of his neck protested the movement. He knew where he was now. Yes, indeed. There was no mistaking the Santa Rosaria jail, not in this lifetime or the next one.

He tried to sit up but only managed to lift his head before the pain sliced through his body. His left side was on fire and the muscles of his shoulders and arms burned like ignited gasoline. He'd really taken a beating from Juan Carlos. He hadn't resisted arrest, at least not enough to deserve a pistol butt across his admittedly thick cranium.

"Montera," he roared in frustration. He held his head in his hands as the reverberations from his foolish act wreaked havoc on his brain. The throbbing behind his eyes was more than enough penance for his "crime." The jail cell just added insult to injury.

"Sleep, Señor Baxter," came the cheerful reply. "You know your *compadres* can't bail you out until we open at eight o'clock."

Deke gritted his teeth in frustration as he glanced up at the small, slitted alcove that served as a window in this hellhole of a place. It was still dark outside. He wondered what time it was, but his watch was, of course, gone. Montera had removed it—for safekeeping as the good captain liked to call it. Sometimes Deke got it back and sometimes he didn't. The watches weren't expensive, and he was too smart to argue with the local authorities in an out-of-the-way place where too many small-minded people had the power to let you rot behind bars indefinitely. He settled himself down to wait.

Damn Bill and his insistence on basing his transport business in the mountain town of Santa Rosaria. He'd pleaded with him for months to change it to one of the bigger, more convenient cities. There was more money to be made there, and more people and more traffic. It meant that a gringo like him didn't stick out like a red parrot in the green jungle every time he stepped onto the street. The cargoes they carried were legitimate these days; they had nothing to hide, no bribes to pay. But old habits died hard with a stubborn guy like his partner. Besides, Bill insisted that life was more pleasant here.

And so they'd nailed him for speeding—again. Whistling along with the Peruvian national anthem on the radio, he'd taken a turn on two wheels at two o'clock in the morning, figuring that all good militia men were safely tucked in their beds, only to find Juan Carlos Montera standing smack in the middle of the road waving his pistol while his sergeant pointed a machine gun right at the windshield where Deke's face made a handy target. He didn't think the wiper would offer much in the way of protection.

Come to think of it, he reflected with a chuckle that jarred his eyeballs and made him wince, maybe he had shown a little disrespect when he slammed on the brakes to avoid the two men, using a heavier-than-needed touch and causing the van to skid right through the front window of the local brothel. He looked down at the bruised knuckles of his right hand. And maybe he had given Juan Carlos more trouble than he should have when the man tried to cart him off to the slammer.

He must have dozed because the next thing he heard was the sound of voices coming down the hallway.

"*Buenos días,* Señor Baxter." That was Montera, damn his cheerful hide. He was smiling broadly as he held up a set of keys and jangled them invitingly.

Deke pulled himself up slowly and painfully until he was in a half-sitting position against the pillows. "Captain Montera," he replied with a stiff nod. The captain was a small, slender man with thick dark hair, sharp black eyes and a proud profile that announced his Spanish ancestry.

"You have been warned before about speeding, no?"

Deke shrugged, then groaned aloud as the skin along the back of his neck tightened in reaction to a shaft of pain that clamped down around his head like a molten iron vise. Gingerly he massaged his scalp. "I think this latest adventure may have cured me."

"We can only pray to the Blessed Virgin that this is so."

He made the sign of the cross, bowing his head respectfully while Deke tried to refrain from snorting in amusement. The only times the good captain called on the Virgin was when he was avoiding his wife or hiding from his formidable mother-in-law.

"Your partner was notified of your latest crime against the peace and serenity of our town," he continued, "and he agreed to pay the fines like the noble gentleman he is." He began pacing back and forth in front of Deke's cell like a caged jaguar even though Deke was the one inside the cage. "However, I am not sure if it is enough to cover all the damages. You see, there was the window and the sidewalk and that beautiful sign Lupita had painted just for the girls...."

"You can have twenty cartons of cigarettes, that's almost a third of what I brought in last night," Deke told him. "Oh, and by the way, keep the watch."

Captain Montera unlocked the door of the cell, swinging it open with a gallant gesture. "Allow me to escort you, *señor.*"

"Thanks, but I think I know the way."

He strode into the office, expecting to find Bill waiting to bawl him out for his carelessness. Instead, Esteban, one of the local kids they sometimes used for errands, stood there.

"Señor Deke!"

"Why aren't you in school?"

The boy raised his eyebrows in innocent bewilderment that Deke knew was carefully calculated to disarm him. These street kids knew how to handle themselves to their own advantage in any situation, and what they didn't know, they faked. "Hermana Maria says I am also learning the ways of buying and selling in the jobs I do for you and Señor Bill."

"What a load of monkey manure." Deke opened the door and gestured the boy to precede him out into the street. "I'm sure Señor Bill paid you well to come over here. It saved him from getting his butt out of bed so early."

Esteban grinned and shrugged. "The good sisters got their cut." His smile faded. "They use the money to buy medicine for the little ones."

Deke ignored the sudden tug at his gut. He knew the boy had lost a younger brother to some illness because of the lack of a simple antibiotic. The Sisters of Mercy did the best they could in difficult times but often it wasn't enough. Anyway, it was none of his business. This particular kid was tough, he would survive.

The boy skipped along beside him, his skinny legs flashing beneath the ragged pair of short pants he wore. Suddenly he reached into the pocket of his shirt. "Oh, here, this came for you." He handed Deke a letter with the familiar U.S.A. postmark.

Deke accepted it reluctantly, thinking it was from his parents. He wrote them occasionally, just to let them know he was still alive and kicking, but he had stretched the truth a touch when he informed them that he had taken up mountain climbing and exploration. He figured it wouldn't hurt them to think he was doing something halfway purposeful with his life, and anyway he had carted that equipment halfway up the side of Sajama for Benito Calavieri and his international crew of climbers last year.

He turned the letter over carefully, then blinked in surprise. "It's from Elvie McConnell," he said, grinning. "He's an old amigo of mine from back home." He stopped to lean against the wall near the bakery, holding the letter in his hands and staring at the cramped handwriting on the envelope. "I wonder what he wants."

"Maybe he wishes to give you money, for more trucks for you and Señor Bill."

Deke laughed as he ruffled the boy's hair. Esteban thought all Americans were wealthy and just looking for ways to spend their piles of cash. "I doubt it, *pequeño*. He's probably scheming something. The two of us were hell on wheels when it came to stirring up trouble."

Deke smiled crookedly, recalling the time he and Elvie had tried to make the old windmill work. He'd ended up with a broken collarbone, but it had been worth it. That was when he had discovered that he didn't have to play by the rules and no one could do a damn thing about it. He didn't have to study, he didn't have to belong to the right clubs in school, he didn't have to play varsity sports. It had been a great relief to stop trying to become something he knew he could never be. He had always felt that Elvie was responsible for that revelation.

He tapped the letter thoughtfully.

Esteban tugged on his sleeve. "Maybe your friend wants to come visit you in Santa Rosaria!"

"I doubt it, 'Stebanito."

The kid shrugged and smiled as Deke reached into his pocket and pulled out the Swiss army knife he always carried with him. Either Juan Carlos had been feeling generous this time or he had missed it. He slit open the letter from Elvie and pulled out the single sheet of paper inside.

Crazy old farmer. They'd been kindred spirits during his days in high school. As he perused the contents he felt the ache of being an outsider as Elvie complained about his stubborn niece, his crazy cousin, his ornery sister. Family ties that Deke had never really experienced in spite of the efforts of his family. In many ways Elvie had been more like kin to him than his own family. Deke had learned a lot about life from Elvie McConnell.

His expression sobered as he continued to read. Elvie was now living with his niece, Sarah Riddle, and was likely to lose his farm to taxes or have it sold out from under him unless he did something about it. The womenfolk had him over a barrel, all right. And now he was hinting at some crazy scheme to find a treasure and buy back his independence.

Deke could understand wanting independence. Elvie McConnell was one of the few people Deke respected because rather than knotting the ropes of affection with conditions, he had wisely given him all the slack he needed. Deke had appreciated that more than he could ever express in words. And now the old guy needed help. Deke wondered if Elvie's plan was wishful thinking. Most get-rich-quick schemes usually were, but it was still worth a chance. Anyway, no matter what the old man wanted from him, he figured he owed him one.

He'd come to accept that life wasn't always fair; that was easy. The difficult part was facing up to the sorry fact that he wasn't even trying anymore to challenge fate and beat the odds. Sure, people tended to worry too much about the future, but that didn't mean he had to waste the days and nights of his life playing Spanish cards and driving a broken-down truck for little profit and even smaller positive effect on the world.

He rubbed the sore muscles at the back of his neck.

"Are you going home, Señor Deke?" the little boy asked wistfully.

"I suppose you could say that. But only for a little while. I'll be back."

Esteban looked stricken. "You won't, either. No one ever returns to Santa Rosaria once they get the chance to escape. And if you go, then Señor Bill will go, too!"

Deke reached out for the boy, not sure what he intended to do but simply reacting to the anguish in his voice. Esteban evaded his hand and took off running down the street, turning the corner and disappearing in a tangle of skinny arms and legs. Deke shrugged. It was a tough world, but the kid would survive. He'd been through worse experiences than one of his gringo friends leaving for a few months.

He wasn't sure how he felt about returning to his hometown like some kind of prodigal son. Still, Justice was simply Justice, a small dot on the map that had never tried to be anything but what it was. He had shut out memories of his earlier life; only occasionally did they manage to play on the screen of his conscious thoughts.

Maybe it wouldn't be so bad to go back and see the old place for a couple of months. He could find out if it had remained the way he remembered it.

Besides, this time he just might be able to do something good there.

"WHAT YOU NEED is a summer project, girl."

Uncle Elvie's innocently delivered statement caught Carly as she stood at the kitchen sink, up to her pushed-up sweater sleeves in suds and dishes.

"You're my summer project," she replied with a small laugh, tossing her dark brown hair out of her eyes with a shake of her head as she turned to face him.

He snorted. "I don't mean you coming home to watch after me," he said in a disgusted voice. "I'm talking about something out of the ordinary, something filled with excitement and the thrill of discovery!" His voice sidled up and down the musical scale in what he probably considered his most irresistible manner.

"You sound like a TV commercial."

"I can promise you more honest-to-goodness living than you'll ever find in that foreign place you're so fond of," he retorted.

She sighed. She was still finding it difficult to adjust to the thought of wasting an entire summer of her life in the small, provincial town where she'd grown up, especially after she'd worked so hard to ensure her escape. Two years spent in the volatile Paris fashion industry had not only sharpened her instinctive flair for line and color, it had also refined her Missouri country edges and she intended to keep it that way.

"I happen to love Paris. There's nowhere like it on the face of this earth," she told him. "Although I suppose you could say the same thing about this place," she added with a cheerful shrug. "Anyway, I don't expect excitement in Justice, Missouri. Looking after you will provide me with all the thrills I need."

"Don't be so sassy-sure of yourself, missy," he told her, shaking a finger in her direction for emphasis. Elvie was a great one for shaking fingers at people. "Your old uncle might have a few surprises up his sleeve."

"Oh, I'm sure you do," she said with a grin. "You've always been full of surprises, Uncle Elvie."

"Along with being full of other, less mentionable things, eh niece?"

She laughed. "I never said that. Blame Mama and Aunt Effie for your bad reputation. They're the ones who both swear they'd rather tangle with a pack of wild geese than try talking sense into you once you've made up your mind. You're not going to give me a hard time while Mama's away, are you?"

"Of course not," he assured her solemnly.

She slanted him a skeptical glance before turning back to her task. She caught a glimpse of her reflection in the window. The skinny, awkward teenager who had stumbled through her salutatorian speech at graduation had disappeared forever, thank goodness, even if some of the people in this town had a hard time realizing that fact. Now her hair was stylishly cut and fell in soft waves around her face, and she dressed with a sophistication originally gleaned from poring over French fashion magazines while in college. She had perfected her style in Paris, that glorious mecca of chic worldliness. She knew that it set her apart from other young women her age in this town, and that suited her just fine. Until she'd spent time abroad, she hadn't known she possessed the courage to be different.

She hadn't relished the thought of looking after her great-uncle Elvie for the summer while her mother took a well-deserved vacation. She'd waited a long time to shake the dust of Justice from her shoes, but she knew she couldn't refuse her mother's plea for assistance. Family roots went deep in Missouri, and it wasn't in Carly to deny her family ties or her background. Besides, the clothing design company she'd been working for had been sold to a huge conglomerate and most of the employees at her level of expertise had been let go, so she was conveniently between jobs at the moment.

Elvie was a trial in any language, no doubt about that. Taking the old man in after he'd had a heart attack had been Sarah Riddle's duty, but caring for her cantankerous uncle during these past nine months as well as teaching school couldn't have been easy. It was now Carly's turn, as a member of the Riddle clan, to give back some of the love she had received so abundantly as a child.

After all, summer didn't last forever, and her beloved city on the Seine was crowded with tourists for the month of August, anyway. She wouldn't be missing anything vital, and she could return in September ready to swing back into her career. She would worry about finding a job and how she was going to scrape together the return fare later, when she was feeling more brilliant.

"Carly, come here and give me a hand, would ya?" Elvie called, interrupting her reverie.

She dried her hands, then followed the sound of his voice into the den. She found him sitting on the floor with a decrepit box of papers in front of him. The name J. James, was scrawled in faded letters across the side. Elvie had probably dragged it over from the farm along with the other battered possessions he had insisted on having by his side when he'd moved in with Sarah.

"What's that?"

"Your summer project."

"*Je pense que non,*" she said, raising her eyebrows in amusement. "That's French for no way."

"Don't go spouting off in that foreign lingo to me, Carly Riddle. You don't even know what's in the dad-blasted box. But I'm gonna let you in on a little secret."

"Please do."

She threw herself down into the nearest chair, a recliner that had been in her family since she was a baby. Its worn corduroy surface and solid hulking shape couldn't come close to the delicate Louis Quinze furniture she'd admired at Versailles. She ran her fingers across one particularly frayed area while she contemplated her uncle. When Elvie was cooking up some scheme it was always better to hear it sitting down.

"So, what's the secret, Uncle Elvie?" she asked calmly.

He pulled a ragged piece of paper from the box. The edges were fragile, and the once-white paper was now brown and faded; Carly thought the entire sheet might disintegrate into powder.

"This here piece of paper is." Elvie chortled in a way that promised trouble. He jiggled the paper around a bit, just for dramatic effect, then reached out to grab her arm, pulling her down onto the floor beside him. "Take a good gander at that," he told her, shoving the paper in front of her face. His voice was full of self-importance.

Carly sighed. She could see that Elvie was working up to embroiling her in something bound to land them both in trouble. Her immediate, instinctive response was to squash the idea before he got rolling with it.

But instead of paying attention to her gut reaction, Carly looked down at the sheet, surprised to find that it showed an old map. She studied it more carefully, unable to stop the thrill of excitement that raced up her spine and settled somewhere in the pit of her stomach. Her hazel eyes glowed, but she automatically banked the fire before Elvie could notice. She'd better be careful not to encourage him until she knew exactly what he was plotting. Still, anyone with an ounce of romance would get excited over a genuine old map. And Carly harbored more romance per square inch than anyone in this town.

"It's a map," she said, stating the obvious.

She reached out a finger to touch the paper. It clearly indicated mountains in one corner and a river flowing through the center, but nothing was labeled and the entire map itself had no legend or title. Near the bottom right-hand corner she noticed a series of strange symbols that might indicate directions. She supposed if she squinted hard enough she could imagine arrows and compass points, but realistically she had to admit it looked more like bird tracks.

"What does it show?" she asked, and this time she couldn't keep the sparkle from her eyes.

"It's a treasure map. See that *X* in the corner there?"

She leaned closer. She hadn't noticed it at first, but sure enough, there was a faintly penciled *X* in the middle of the mountains. "Yes, I see it."

"It shows the location of the cave where Jesse James stashed some of the loot from his last batch of bank robberies. And it's on *my* property!"

"You're pulling my leg," she said, laughing in relief. He'd really had her going for a minute there. She looked up, her laughter abruptly halted when she saw his face. "You're not pulling my leg? How do you know for certain?"

"Because it's been handed down in my family since old Jesse gave it to my grandfather, that's why."

"Oh."

"He did a favor for Jesse once. Actually, it was his mother Granddad helped that time after someone planted a bomb in her house, hoping to take Jesse out. Lost her arm, too, she did."

"Oh, poor woman! That's awful."

"That's right. And you know what else is awful?" He leaned over until he was nose to nose with her. "My situation, that's what! I want my dad-blasted farm back. That heart attack business that laid me flat as a toad under a rock is over and done with. I'm all recovered now. I know your ma's a fine Christian woman. She took me in and I appreciate it. But the time has come for me to make my move."

Carly scrambled to her feet. "You know what the doctors said, Uncle Elvie. You shouldn't do anything strenuous until they're certain your heart is functioning properly. You can't go back to farming now."

"The blasted hell I can't," he roared. "Pardon my French." He grinned at his own joke, then pointed a finger at her and waved it around in bold slashes as he continued his harangue, his face growing more florid with every syllable. "I can work the farm if I get me a hired hand. I always fancied myself a boss man, anyway, so now I'll get my chance. Hell in a hand basket, maybe I'll even hire two hands. Now, to do that I'll need me some cold hard cash. That's where you come in, missy. I know I'm too old to go digging through the tunnels of some scrabbly old cave, but you're not."

"Please calm down, Uncle Elvie," she advised him gently, touching his arm in what she hoped was a soothing gesture, trying not to show the panic she was feeling at the sight of his agitation. He wasn't supposed to become excited. "You're getting carried away with this thing. I don't think I'm exactly qualified to go exploring caves."

"You won't have to do it alone, niece! I've asked Ed Baxter's boy to come and give you a hand."

Carly's mouth dropped open in astonishment. "Oh, no," the words slipped out on a whisper of breath. "Not him."

"Why not? If anybody has a sense of adventure in his blood, it's Deke. He likes to get things done."

"He also likes to blow things up, in case you've forgotten. Remember when he blew up the school yard swings? Or what about that time he tried to dynamite the Black River? That was something he *got done* all right."

"Yeah, buddy. But he was just a kid then. And he did it for a good cause." He chuckled. "Imagine trying to divert the river so the Kittermans would have water for their garden. Anyway, I hear he's a real explorer now, climbing mountains and such like that."

"Climbing mountains is not the same thing as going down into a cave. You have to know what you're doing. People can get lost and die in an unexplored cave. Don't you remember Francie Dilly? She got lost in Devil's Cavern on that Girl Scout trip and it took them three days to find her."

Even as she argued, Carly's mind was racing. It all sounded romantic and exciting, tramping around the countryside looking for traces of outlaws and their loot, but she knew the reality would be quite different. Her career as a Girl Scout had only lasted until her troop had decided to camp out on Merrimec Mountain. That was when she discovered she was not destined to conquer the great outdoors. She must be a throwback to some blue-blood aristocratic ancestor because the pioneer blood of her foremothers did not flow in her veins. She'd tasted grit between her teeth for a week after she'd returned and had vowed to budget a clean hotel with running water and toilet facilities into any further travel plans she ever made.

Besides, she had a responsibility to her uncle's health. She'd promised her mother she would keep him calm and out of trouble this summer, and Jesse James, secret caves and a mysterious map were not soothing concepts.

Then there was Deacon Baxter. Surely he was too busy to come back to Justice. He hadn't been back since the day they'd handed him his diploma. She'd even heard a rumor that he'd been a half credit short for graduation so the school board had given him a grade for customizing his motorcycle. It was the only subject he'd ever gotten an *A* in. The last thing she needed was Deke hanging around and spurring Elvie on to new heights of foolish, wild behavior.

Elvie ignored her arguments. "Deke'll figure everything out," he insisted. "What's so danged difficult? Mountains, caves—it's all just dirt and rocks, isn't it?"

"That's one way of looking at it, I suppose," she said, stifling a groan. Deke was not the soothing presence Elvie needed in his life right now. She bit her lip as she considered a middle path. "Maybe you and I can try to figure out the map together. Then we wouldn't need to bother Deke."

"Shoot fire, Carly, that won't work, neither. I need both of you. Deke'll have to have some help when he explores the cave. You can't send a man down into the cold, dark earth without having a friendly body to shine the flashlight."

Carly grimaced. "Your logic is flawed, Uncle. How can you contemplate running an entire farm, if you're not even capable of holding a flashlight? Not that it matters, because I refuse to be a friendly body to Deacon Baxter and I can't allow you to be one, either."

"Now Carly, you know you don't mean that."

She rolled her eyes and shook her head. This had gone far enough. It was time for her to stiffen her resolve and do what was right for Elvie, even if he didn't see that it was for his own good. "Yes, I most certainly do mean that. You know Mama would kill me if I let you run off on some crazy treasure hunt. If she ever gets wind that we're even talking about this, she'll skin my hide. The subject is closed. You've got a good home now, your life is all settled and that's that." She looked him straight in the eye. "I can find things for you to do if you're bored."

"I ain't bored," he grumbled and shuffled out of the room in a sulk.

Carly blew out her breath in relief as she watched him leave, her expression filled with both sympathy and trepidation. She knew Elvie hadn't given up, not by a long shot. He was only regrouping his forces, planning for the next assault on her logic and her emotions since his first attempt hadn't panned out to his satisfaction.

Playing around with treasure maps didn't bother her, but the thought of Elvie huffing and puffing his way around the hills of Justice, his heart struggling to keep pace with the heat, scared the stuffing out of her. And here she'd thought a body couldn't get into trouble in Justice, Missouri, a town of 3,022 residents whose main street didn't even boast a traffic light.

She sighed again. But of course those visions of trouble-free living precluded such hardheaded male specimens as Elvie McConnell and Deacon Baxter, especially when you hitched the pair of them in tandem. Deke's image flashed into her memory, or at least his image as he'd appeared in high school almost fifteen years ago. It still had the power to elicit a reaction from her, part disapproval of his rebellious ways and part admiration for his irrepressible spirit in the face of an often stifling small-town environment.

He'd been a rebel all right, the wildest kid in school, and he had caused trouble for everyone, especially his teachers and the high school principal. He'd even been arrested twice by the police, once for defacing the walls of the gymnasium and once for knocking over all the mailboxes on the east side of town. The shopkeepers on Main Street had been particularly glad to see the back of him; they'd insisted that Deke shoplifted in their stores on a regular basis, but the allegations had never been proved to anyone's satisfaction. Carly had always felt sorry for his parents, Ed and Opal Baxter, who seemed much too decent to deserve such antics from their son.

She turned to head toward her room, where the latest French fashion magazines awaited her attention. Just because Elvie had written to him didn't mean anything, she assured herself. Chances were good that he wouldn't even show up.

Chapter Two

The grapevine of Justice still worked, Carly thought with a wry smile as she hung up the phone. She had taken her mother's position as one of the hubs of the local information network, and she was now the proud possessor of the news that Deke was back in Justice. Even before she'd had a chance to take her first sip of coffee, Mrs. Hepplewhite had been on the line, tripping over the words in her haste to elaborate on all the lurid details of "that ungrateful Baxter boy's" return to the town of his youth.

According to Mrs. Hepplewhite, Deke hadn't actually done anything that could get him arrested so far. But, her underlying tone implied, he'd only just cruised into town early this morning and the day was still young. He still looked like a hooligan, she had assured Carly, and he still drove that motorcycle. Lowering her voice to a self-important whisper, the older woman had reported that Deacon had actually had the nerve to seat himself at the counter of Jan's Family Restaurant for breakfast when everyone knew that Jan had personally escorted him to the door sometime during the first week of his sophomore year, telling him never to darken it again.

Carly chuckled to herself. She supposed it was ironically fitting that Mrs. Hepplewhite be the one to tell her. After all, the woman had played a small but vital role that one time she'd landed herself in trouble because of Deke Baxter.

She allowed the memory to come flooding back. Much to her chagrin she found that she could still visualize everything about that fine Missouri spring day when Deke had pulled alongside her on his shiny black motorcycle. He'd been wearing black pants and boots along with a white shirt and a worn leather jacket from the secondhand store in town. His hair was dark blond and too long to be respectable, although secretly Carly had found it attractive.

But it was his eyes that had caught her own and held them for endless moments. They were a bright blue and they blazed with untamed energy. He was the bad boy come to life, and Carly was no different from any other female in the face of all that forceful maleness sitting astride his bike. He straddled it as though it were the wildest untamed stallion on the range, controlling it with a flex of his thigh muscles, revving up the engine with a casual flick of his wrist. She hadn't been able to look away.

"You look like you could use some loosening up," he said to her in a voice that sounded wickedly enticing to the shy, awkward girl she was. "Want a ride?"

She just stared at him and he laughed, a wicked-sounding scary male laugh that made her think of back seats and hot kisses even though she had never experienced either one. He held out his hand, and in a trance she grasped it. When he pulled her onto the back of the bike, guiding her hands around his lean waist and laughing at her over his shoulder, she had forgotten every ordinary thing about her life and had tumbled headfirst into a movielike fantasy. He smelled of leather and cigarettes and some deeper, more elusive masculine scent that set her pulse racing even harder.

He roared off down the street, weaving in and out of the side streets and around Joiner's Drugstore before skidding to a halt in front of the five-and-dime store. It was her first real taste of freedom, and it was a heady experience to discover that suddenly nothing else mattered except the wind in her hair and the warm sun beating down on the top of her head.

She couldn't have been on the bike more than fifteen minutes. But in a small town like Justice probably eighty percent of the population had noticed her fall from grace as her mother later called it. The best student in the freshman class had no business riding around with the senior class troublemaker. But in those moments Carly hadn't cared that this boy flouted every grown-up in town. She only knew that his recklessness had touched something inside her. She wasn't sure what it was he needed to prove, but in that moment she bought it, hook, line and sinker. She got off the bike in the same trance in which she'd accepted the ride in the first place.

"Miss Carly Riddle," he said, his deep voice mocking her shyness. She glanced up quickly, noting that his dancing blue eyes were filled with mischief as they gleamed at her. "How old are you now?"

"Fourteen. Fifteen in five months." She straightened to her full height, putting her line of vision level with his chin.

He looked her up and down with the casual arrogance any eighteen-year-old male could easily summon in the presence of a younger, inexperienced female. "And never been kissed, I'll bet."

She blushed because it was true, and then she did something quite out of character for her. She lied about it. "Yes I have," she told him.

Something in his eyes flared into life, as though her words had provoked a challenge. "If that's true, then you won't mind if I do this," he said.

Before she even knew what was happening he had swooped down to cover her mouth with his. And it was a real kiss, too, like the kind she'd seen on television and in the movies. His lips moved against hers for what seemed like a small eternity but couldn't have been more than ten or fifteen seconds. They were soft and tasted good, a combination of tobacco and hot-blooded male that surprised her into immobility. It was scary in a delicious, forbidden sort of way, but she was too embarrassed to really enjoy it, knowing that they were standing in full view on Main Street where anyone could be watching them.

"I think you have real potential, Miss Carly," he said to her with a devilish grin, the tone of his voice still mocking but not with cruelty. "You're welcome to look me up anytime you want more. I don't know about you, but I can always use the practice."

He revved up the bike until she thought it was going to explode and then peeled off down the street, leaving a nicely defined strip of tire rubber as a gift for

the town fathers. Mr. Dooley, who owned the five-
and-dime, had come out of his store to stare after the
renegade.

"I'm surprised at you, Carly," he said in a disap-
proving voice before turning on his heel to return to his
customers.

She'd been a little surprised herself. By the time
she'd finished growing up, Deke had long since left
town, but by then she was old enough to realize that
men like Deacon Baxter would always attract nice
women like her, partly because of the curiosity factor
and partly because every human being harbored at
least one irrational impulse.

She took another sip of her coffee, running her finger around the rim as she wondered what he had really thought of her on that long-ago day. She wasn't
even sure why he had kissed her; she certainly didn't
fit his requirements for female companionship, being
neither hot-looking nor particularly fun-loving. Deke
had always chased girls like Sherry O'Sullivan, who
had developed incredible breasts by the age of fourteen and who wasn't averse to necking with a boy out
at Lake Tapahoe.

Carly squirmed in her chair as she recalled some of
the graphic scenarios her fanciful teenage mind had
created using Deke's kiss as the starting point. Feeling the need for movement, she got up to walk across
the kitchen and stand by the window.

There was no need to feel embarrassed, she told
herself firmly. After all, he had been the first boy to
kiss her. The shock of such an encounter in any girl's
life was bound to make an impression. Knowing Deke,
he'd probably been hoping she would slap his face or

something equally dramatic that would shock the older generation and enhance his reputation.

Thank goodness those painful days of adolescence were all in the past. She'd never harbored any intention of falling in love with a local boy and settling down in Justice. Everyone had a guiding principle, and hers had become her quest to experience as many of the finer things life had to offer as she could. Elegant dining, art and music, literature, all the things that made human intercourse beautiful and refined, these were the ideals she would always pursue. She had dined on caviar and sipped champagne in Paris, and she would never return to munching pretzels and chugging beer in Justice.

She was about to reheat the remnants of her coffee in the microwave when she heard the motorcycle roar into the front yard. She raced to the living room in time to see it skid into a turn James Dean would be proud of, just so its rider could neatly park it alongside the rhododendron bush. She closed her eyes in dismay. He was here already. Her blood began to pump in her veins, and she placed her hand against her heart as though she needed to keep it from jumping out of her chest.

Elvie's distress signal had been received and acknowledged. Who would have ever thought that Deke would go out of his way to help anyone, least of all an old man he hadn't seen in years? She knew that Elvie had always had a way with him, but it must have gone deeper than anyone had ever realized.

No matter now, Deke Baxter was about to plunk himself down on her doorstep, ready to aid and abet his old buddy. Carly felt like locking all the doors and windows against this new threat to her uncle's—and her own—peace of mind. She had finally managed to get him down to only mentioning Jesse James once or twice a day; she didn't need reinforcements to turn up now.

She peered out the window, careful not to disturb the curtain. Times must really be tough when Deacon Baxter had to return to Justice to stir up some action. Had the mountain climbing business gone into a slump? She pushed open the screen door and stepped out onto the porch, her arms automatically crossing against her chest in a gesture that contained hints of both indignation and self-protection.

Deke removed his helmet and cradled it in his arms as he gazed up at her from the back of the bike. She knew she looked different from the way he probably remembered her. The material of her loose floral trousers clung softly to her hips and thighs. The yellow blouse she'd paired them with was shirred and feminine. To offset all the sweetness, she wore chunky earrings and a boldly modern watch. She'd caught part of her dark hair with a pretty clip to keep it out of her eyes in anticipation of the chores ahead.

When she wore clothes like these, she could still imagine she was strolling along the Champs-Elysées, watching the crowds of people hurrying to their destinations. At least it was chivalrous of Deke to catch her looking her best, but in spite of her shine of sophistication, he still managed to skew her equilibrium.

Still, she wasn't about to back down now. She self-consciously smoothed the waistband of her trousers, relaxing her arms at the same time. More than likely

Deke Baxter read body language as a sideline—it went along with having a diploma in making women like her feel uncomfortable.

"Good morning, Carly Riddle." He was already grinning as he remained sprawled on the back of that infernal black-and-chrome machine, not even granting her the courtesy of dismounting so he could speak to her properly.

"Deke." She inclined her head in the most token of greetings propriety allowed in circumstances like these.

"Want a ride?"

"Very funny. I have things to do." She didn't try to hide the disapproval in her voice even as her heart jumped at the fact that he remembered the ride he had once offered to a shy young girl.

"What kind of things?" He tilted his head and the sun glinted off the dark gold strands of hair that framed his tanned face. Sunglasses hid his eyes, but Carly knew he was amused by her.

"Things in the house. Laundry. Vacuuming."

"You shouldn't dress up so pretty if you expect me to believe that."

"I didn't expect you to believe anything except that I'm not going anywhere."

"Come on, Carly. You did it once before and didn't come to any harm that I recall." He pulled his sunglasses off so he could look her up and down in a more leisurely fashion. "I'm surprised you're still hanging around this one-horse town. You sure don't look as though you fit in here anymore."

She couldn't help smiling. "That's a real compliment coming from you. But I haven't been hanging around Justice. I've been living in Paris for the last

two-and-a-half years. Mom took a little vacation so
I'm just here temporarily."

She tried not to stare at him but couldn't help herself. She might have changed a bit since her Justice
days, but Deke seemed radically altered to the core. He
looked older than his thirty-two years. Mountain
climbing must be a harsh occupation.

His tanned complexion showed him to be a man
who spent a good deal of time outside. It highlighted
the squint lines that were deeply etched around his
eyes. He still wore his hair long, but the color now held
varying shades of gold and pure, pale yellow. The
combination of his dark skin and streaked blond hair
only emphasized the blueness of his eyes. They still
blazed with life but had been tempered with experience. The overall effect was even more potent than it
had been in high school.

"I'm here for the summer, too," he informed her
with a sideways glance. "So why don't you come for
a ride? It's too beautiful a day to worry about chores
that will be there when you get back." He gestured
broadly with an arm. "I must admit that the thought
of your lovely arms wrapped around me is a thrill."
He raised his eyebrows. "I'll bet we can still scandal-
ize the good folks of Justice."

"I'll leave the scandalizing to you."

He shrugged. "Is Elvie around?"

"He's taking a nap at the moment."

"A nap?" The unfeigned surprise in his voice made
Carly smile.

"A nap. The man is now seventy years old in case
you've lost track. He gets up at five, so by eleven

o'clock he usually lies down. Just to recharge his batteries, as he insists."

She came down the steps to stand at the bottom, her right arm wrapped around the railing. Lowering her voice, she continued in a whisper. "Anyway, he doesn't need to see you. You'll only encourage him in this crazy plan of his, and he's not well enough to start up with all this treasure business. I've talked him out of it."

Deke frowned as he considered her. "Is he senile yet?" he asked, his eyes narrowing to focus intently on her face.

"What?"

"I said, Is he senile yet?"

"Of course not." Carly frowned as she rubbed her fingers against the warm iron beneath them. "He had a heart attack, not a stroke or anything that affected his brain. He's as sharp as he ever was."

"And that's pretty sharp as we both have good reason to know. The way I see it, you have no business trying to run his life for him. He's a grown man, and he should be able to do whatever the hell he wants without you coddling him."

"I'm not coddling him," Carly retorted indignantly. "I am simply following the doctor's orders." Her lips tightened in exasperation as she realized how defensive she sounded.

"And who asked you to do that? Did Elvie ask you to be his guardian angel?"

Carly didn't flinch. "He didn't, but my mother did," she said quietly.

He leaned forward, his expression serious and earnest as his eyes met and held hers. "Take it from someone who learned the hard way, doctors don't know everything. Sometimes shooting for a dream heals people faster than being cautious and following the rules. It certainly gives them a reason to live. Elvie has a dream right now, and I think you should let him hold on to it.''

''Well, thank you for that enlightening bit of philosophy,'' she retorted, angry because she knew that deep down inside, part of her agreed with him, probably because she'd just lived through three weeks of feeling like Scrooge at his meanest while she worked to wean Elvie away from his plan.

Deke had always been persuasive. Because she knew that and because she felt her own stance softening, she forced herself to argue for the other side. ''He needs to face the facts, not chase after pie-in-the-sky booty from an outlaw who's been dead for a hundred years or more. If there's anything left of this stash of money, don't you think someone would have found it by now?''

He shrugged. ''Maybe yes, maybe no,'' he said softly, leaning forward.

Carly tried to ignore the feelings his proximity was generating inside her. She was more aware of him now than she had ever been as a naive fifteen-year-old. A lock of his hair moved in the breeze, and she decided it was probably the softest thing about him. Only a fool could miss the controlled power evident in every muscle and sinew of the man, but surely that should have no effect on the way she intended to conduct this conversation with him.

''Anyway, that's beside the point,'' he continued softly. ''Just the fact that he's trying to do something about his circumstances and not just letting life happen to him is enough to make this whole scheme worthwhile. Believe me, Carly, I know what I'm talking about here."

"He needs to take it easy for a while," she insisted.

"Not if I know Elvie. If you try to thwart him on this, he's just going to end up doing it behind your back and then he really will get hurt."

"He can't do it behind my back unless you help him," she pointed out with an exasperated shake of her head. In spite of her inclination to agree with him, Carly still felt that Deke was taking this all too lightly. "It's not that I want to spoil his fun, but I *won't* put his life in jeopardy. My mother asked me to watch over him and I intend to do just that." She knew she sounded self-righteous, but she intended to make her point clearly.

She looked up to find him gazing intently at her as he chewed on a long piece of grass he had plucked from a patch growing alongside the porch. "No offense to your mother or you, but only Elvie knows what's good for Elvie. Now, I can't say what kind of things we're going to get into on this deal, but it's still his decision."

"He might get hurt. He's talking about going down into some cave." She only flinched a little at the lie. Actually he'd wanted her and Deke to handle that particular segment of his dirty work.

"You're worrying about something that hasn't even happened yet. Besides, I'm not going to let him do anything I don't think he's capable of. That's what I'm here for, to handle the hard parts."

He moved his helmet to the back of the bike before sliding a long leg over the black leather seat. She tried not to notice the tight fit of his well-worn jeans as he strode to the bottom of the porch steps. His wide-legged stance, the way his leather jacket made a blatant statement about his don't-give-a-damn attitude, his challenging blue eyes, all these things made her wish that she could point a gun at him and say, "Don't come any closer, mister, or I'll put a bullet right between your eyes." The heroines in those Western movies Elvie was so fond of often did it, not that it always got the desired results.

Deke was always one to head for the edge just to see how far he could go. That might be okay as a choice when you were young, but Elvie was no youngster anymore. Just because Deke had climbed to the top of some mountain among other exploits didn't mean Elvie had to try to copy his reckless philosophy of living.

"Give me some credit, Carly," Deke went on in that raspy voice that had always sounded so sinful. "And give some to Elvie. We're not going to do anything stupid."

"Who's stupid?" Elvie poked his head through the open window to call out. He looked from Carly to Deke, oblivious of the tense conversation he had interrupted, then abruptly pulled his head back in. Moments later he tramped onto the porch, grinning from ear to ear as he hitched up his suspenders. "Deke, you rangy, mangy son of a gun!"

"Elvie." Deke grinned as he watched Elvie come down the stairs, hands outstretched. The two men shook hands and Elvie clapped Deke on the back, causing a groan from the younger man.

"What's this? Am I still too strong for you, boy?"

Deke laughed. "I got into a small scuffle with a couple of the local boys down in Incaland. They were better armed than I was. Got a little banged up, but nothing time won't heal."

"Carly's got some great liniment, and she gives a fantastic massage to go along with it. Does wonders for a body's soreness."

"I just might take her up on it," he said with a wicked smile in her direction. "If she doesn't murder me first."

"Carly wouldn't hurt a fly, would you, honey?"

"I wouldn't be so sure of that." Deke shrugged nonchalantly. "If looks could kill, I think I'd be playing a harp somewhere right now."

"I don't think harp-playing is exactly what you'd be doing," Carly murmured sweetly.

Elvie ignored her to get right down to the business at hand. "So did you two decide how you're gonna tackle finding Jesse's hidden cave?" He noticed Deke's puzzled expression. "I'll bet Carly didn't even show you the dad-blasted map yet."

"Carly has the map?" he asked, interest thickening his voice.

"Sure, Deke. Didn't she tell ya? She's part of the expedition! I got it all planned, son. You didn't think I was hauling this old carcass all over the county, did ya?"

"Uncle Elvie, I told you I wasn't getting involved in this thing." Carly tried to keep the total exasperation she felt out of her voice, although she couldn't help monitoring Deke's reaction from the corner of her eye. "And neither are you."

"Aw, Carly, now you sound just like your mother," Elvie protested. "A fine woman, but a royal pain in the anatomy when it comes to doing anything not sanctioned by the Ladies' Auxiliary. Don't be an old lady, Carly. I was counting on you to see my side of this." He turned to Deke with a chuckle. "My Carly's real good at seeing both sides of any issue. I always said she'd make one hell of a lousy lawyer because she'd be arguing for both the defense and the prosecution."

"I'm glad to hear she's so fair," Deke replied.

"Now, just a minute," Carly interrupted the male collusion, her hands on her hips as she looked from one to the other. "I absolutely refuse to be flattered into doing something I don't think is right."

"Then we'll have to work on changing your definition of what's right, won't we, Elvie?"

"Yeah, buddy. Come on in, Deke, and I'll show you what I've got." Elvie waved Deke into the house.

Carly huffed a minute, then decided to effect a strategic retreat while she thought about her options. She knew what her mother would want her to do. Her mother had always seen things clearly and never dithered over issues. Carly backed around the screen door into the house and fled to the kitchen.

As she leaned against the refrigerator, she listened to Elvie explaining the history of the map and what the plan of attack should be. All she heard from Deke were murmurs of affirmation and agreement. She was definitely outgunned. If he hadn't shown up to add reinforcement, Elvie would have been shut down before he'd even gotten his motor running.

The bottom line was that she stood alone against two hardheaded men who didn't understand the meaning of the word impossible. Deke was not on the side of reason and common sense and never had been. She couldn't appeal to his better nature since he didn't have one. So what was she supposed to do?

She blew out the breath she'd been holding, then walked to the kitchen window to look out across Riddle Hill. Her family had been around Justice for a long time, but precious little good her lineage did her in this situation. She just couldn't let Elvie go wandering around the hills of Justice, even if she had to stop him by going out there and toting a pick and shovel herself. And yet she knew that Deke had a valid point when he said that Elvie would simply try to do his treasure hunting behind her back. She drew aside the yellow curtain and peered out across the back porch and into the grassy backyard where the old stone birdbath sat.

If she called her mother, Carly knew she would rush home and put a halt to all of Elvie's plans. But she just didn't have the heart to do that. As far as she could tell, there was only one way to handle this. She simply had to play along with the idea and hope that the three of them had little success. After all, they had to find the cave before they could go down into it, and from the looks of that map it wasn't going to be as easy as Elvie was talking it up to be.

She let the curtain fall back into place as her plan coalesced. If it ever actually became necessary to go inside the cave, she would very calmly inform Deke that she simply couldn't do it, that she'd always had a terrible case of cave-o-phobia or whatever the correct psychological term for it was. If she needed more ammunition she could easily invent an allergic reaction to stalagmites or stalactites or whatever those iciclelike formations were called. Even Deke couldn't be hardhearted enough to force her to crawl into some bat-infested cave with hang-ups like those. And he certainly wouldn't be able to go without backup assistance, would he? She knew nothing about caves, but she prayed it was so. And then, by the time he found someone else, summer would be over, her mother would be home and everything would be taken out of her hands.

She bit her lip, her hazel eyes gleaming with determination. There was more than one way to pluck a chicken, she thought, as she considered further. It was up to her to apply the brakes to this two-man juggernaut. Elvie was right about her tendency to vacillate; she'd always found it difficult to stand irrevocably on any one side of an issue, especially when someone came along to argue the other guy's side of things. Just knowing that her uncle had his heart so set on finding Jesse James's loot softened her resistance enough as it was. Even now a little voice inside her head wondered what the harm in it was, especially if Deke did all the manual labor.

Drawing a deep breath, she turned toward the living room. It wouldn't hurt to find out what was going on in the meantime. Burying her head in the sand might be tempting, but it couldn't erase the fact that she was responsible for Elvie.

She found them bent over the map which now lay across the coffee table, Elvie's graying head and Deke's blond one almost touching in deep consultation.

"Hi," she announced brightly. "How about some lemonade?"

Elvie turned accusing eyes toward her. "How about a little consideration for age and wisdom?" he snorted indignantly. He was still angry with her.

"All right."

"Does that mean you're going to help?" Elvie's pale hazel eyes brightened immediately.

"I didn't say that exactly. But I suppose there's no harm in talking about it for the time being," Carly said with a casual shrug, still unwilling to endorse their plans fully. She could see that Deke watched her with a speculative expression on his face.

"What happens when talk turns to action?" he asked in a low, lazy drawl. He leaned back against the couch cushions, looking annoyingly at home.

Her smile was strained. "I guess we'll cross that bridge when we come to it, won't we?"

He shrugged in a way that was quickly becoming familiar to her. "Either that or you'll blow the damn bridge up before we even get there."

"Now Deke, give the poor girl a chance, can't you? It's a start, she's trying." He turned to Carly. "You won't regret it, niece, you can bet the farm on that." He slapped his thigh. "Ha, bet the farm on it, that's exactly what I'm doing, ain't it?"

Carly felt a sharp stab of guilt somewhere in her chest. She knew what it was like to want something that everyone else said you could never attain. After all, *she* had succeeded against the odds. But this wasn't the same type of situation, she assured herself firmly. She had to do what was best for her uncle no matter how difficult it became. She was taking a sensible course and had no cause to feel like Benedict Arnold.

"We'd better swear her to secrecy, don't you think, Elvie?" Deke's voice was soft and full of implications that didn't bear further examination. "Not that you can't trust your own niece, but there's a proper way to go about a project like this."

"Of course, of course." Elvie quickly followed the lead Deke handed him without a second thought. Carly repressed the urge to glare at Deke; it wouldn't help her in the long run, and besides, she didn't want to give him the satisfaction of knowing he had rattled her.

"I hope I don't need to sign in blood," she said lightly. "I faint at the sight of it."

"Naw." Elvie chuckled gleefully. "Deke's just talking about the honorable man's way of doing business, with a handshake and a promise, that's all. It makes everything official. I know you wouldn't do anything to hurt your old uncle."

"Of course she wouldn't," Deke hastened to assure him even as his look to her implied otherwise. It wasn't her imagination that supplied the sarcastic tone in his deep voice, either.

Elvie cleared his throat before explaining. "We made a pledge to find Jesse's loot, come hell or high water. And then we shook on it. Now that you're gonna help us, we'll really be a team."

He held out his hand to her, grinning widely. His trust and affection for her was almost palpable. She glanced at Deke, who continued to watch her. She knew it was useless to wish herself anyplace else, but she couldn't help doing it, anyway. But even after she blinked her vision clearer, she was still staring at Elvie's outstretched hand.

"Come hell or high water," Deke pledged softly as he extended his hand to her as well, his blue eyes gleaming.

Carly stared at both hands, one gnarled and workworn, the other long, lean and covered with calluses and scars. *He knows,* she thought, a sinking feeling washing over her and settling in the pit of her stomach. *He knows I'm still undecided about wanting to help and he's trapped me into this sham of a ritual because he thinks he can hold me to it.*

A shaft of anger welled up in her. Well, I've got news for him, she decided. All's fair when the health and well-being of someone you love are at stake, and after everything's said and done, I'm still going to follow my conscience.

She reached out to shake first Elvie's hand, then Deke's. She could feel that her smile contained more bravado than was called for, but she refused to dwell on it. "Come hell or high water," she repeated the vow, placing her own meaning on the phrase. She looked for signs of stress or agitation on Elvie's face, but he looked like a happy child on Christmas morning.

Deke gave her hand a meaningful squeeze which she blithely ignored. He wasn't going to badger her into abandoning her common sense. They had totally different motivations, and she couldn't count on him to ever understand hers.

"Well, let's get down to it. I'll go fetch the rest of what I've got, including my Granddaddy's diary." Elvie hauled himself off the sofa and shuffled out of the room.

Carly listened as he trudged up the stairs with his familiar heavy tread. Finally, when she knew she could stall no longer, she met Deke's eyes.

He was waiting for her. "How long before you break your word, I wonder," he asked in an almost philosophical manner. His blue gaze pierced right through her. "I'll be ready for it, don't you worry, Carly. You talk a good game, but your eyes tell me you're lying."

She knew it was probably hopeless, but she tried bluffing, anyway. "What are you talking about?"

"You mean to deter us in any way you can, don't you?"

Carly felt a swift surge of anger infusing every nerve ending. What gave him the right to second guess her? He didn't know her well enough to understand how she felt.

"That's not true," she said in a carefully controlled voice. "I'm only trying to be sensible about things. A little caution is needed in a situation like this, and since neither you nor Uncle Elvie are very heavily endowed with that quality, I've appointed myself to provide it."

"I thought you were different, that you had changed on the inside as much as you have on the outside," he continued in that annoying philosophizing tone.

"Look who's talking. I don't see anyone trying to pin a good conduct medal to your chest."

"Maybe they will after this summer."

He leaned forward, his elbows on his knees in an earnest pose as he smiled appealingly, directly into her eyes. Carly assured herself that that's all it was, a pose. The man was way off base if he thought she would suddenly buy into the vision he was presenting of overcoming all the odds until they attained glorious victory. That only happened in the movies.

"Have you really looked at this thing clearly?" he asked. "What's the harm in helping the old man enjoy what's left of his life? He won't actually be getting himself into any kind of danger, not if we're both around to help him. Between the two of us, we can make sure he doesn't come to any harm. In fact, we can assure that he has a damned good time, no matter what the outcome.

"And suppose we do find something?" Deke continued. "Then he'll be able to do what he likes without asking anybody. He'll be free. That's what he's trying to buy now, his freedom, the freedom that he's had all his life and that you and your mother have conspired to take away from him."

"I didn't conspire to do any such thing," she protested in a horrified whisper. It really sounded terrible when he put it into terms like that.

"Then you're an accessory after the fact."

He reached across the couch to grab her arm, tugging at it until her face was only inches away from his. The soft lamplight assisted by the shaft of sunlight coming through the window illuminated his features sharply, bringing out the clean strength of his bone structure.

"Will you please stop twisting things?" she cried, both furious and distressed by his accusations. "I didn't plan on Elvie having a heart attack. I didn't plot to take away his farm. Sometimes things just happen and you have to accept them."

"That's the whole point of what I'm trying to say. You don't have to accept anything. That's just plain defeatist talk, and I don't think you should be infecting Elvie with it and spoiling his fun."

"Is that all you can think of, fun?" she hissed, jerking her arm out of his grip. She was totally on the defensive, wondering why she was even bothering to argue against an opponent as formidable as Deke. She knew she should just give in gracefully, but he kept managing to coax the more argumentative side out of her usually even-tempered nature.

"What would you rather think about?" he asked sarcastically. "Death? Taxes? Personally, I prefer contemplating the chance that Jesse James did hide some money in a cave, as unlikely as that might be. Especially if it makes my old friend Elvie happy."

Carly threw out her hands in defeat. "All right, all right. You win. Just please stop hammering at me."

Deke slid closer to her and grabbed her hands, taking them both in his one larger one and using his free hand to brush her dark hair back.

"You won't be sorry, Carly," he murmured softly, turning her head with gentle fingers so that her eyes were forced to gaze into his. He slipped one arm around her. "I realize that you want Elvie to be happy. Just give this thing a chance. Give me a chance. Who knows, maybe in a week or two we'll discover that the map is a fake. Or maybe we'll all end up as rich as kings. In either case, what's the harm.''

"He might get too excited. Have another heart attack,'' she said, hating herself for continuing to point out obstacles.

"I think it's more likely he'll have a stroke worrying about how to get his farm back if you try to stop him. Even if we don't succeed, he'll know that he tried his best, and that's a good thing for a man's pride.''

Carly gazed up into his handsome face. She couldn't help breathing in his masculine scent, being held so close to his body. His arm was still around her. She wasn't surprised to note how good she felt in the circle of his embrace. At least this time the good townspeople weren't watching her, so she felt free to fully savor the experience of being soothed by Deacon Baxter without guilt or judgment getting in the way. It was even nicer than she had ever imagined.

It was also very exciting, and it caught her off guard. Although she had tried hard to imitate the carefree French attitude about life and men while she'd been in Paris, the habits of her youth were hard to shake off, especially now that she found herself back in Justice. Good old American prudence still held the upper hand.

She jumped up from the couch, smoothing down her blouse and unconsciously wetting her lips. The French had a word for the way she felt and probably looked: *gauche.* Just saying the word to herself brought forth waves of the old insecurity she'd dealt with in high school. She tried to rationalize her awkwardness. Why shouldn't he make her feel like an awkward fifteen-year-old when that was the way she remembered herself in relation to him? Well, it simply had to stop. Just because she was home didn't mean she had to revert to childhood behaviors she had long since discarded.

"Listen, Deke, let's not argue about this anymore. I've already said okay. I see your point, and I'm willing to go along with your plans as long as it doesn't endanger Elvie's health. If we both watch out for him, everything should be all right." She grinned as she walked over to the drapes, opening them wider to let in more light. "In fact, I'm feeling so generous that I'll even let you be the one to explain it to my mother when she comes home."

"You're still nervous around me," he murmured in soft amazement as he eased himself to his feet. Although he remained across the room from her, she could feel the strength of his will engulfing her. Why couldn't he let it be? What did he want from her? Wasn't her capitulation on the treasure business enough? "I'm not going to pounce on you the way I did on Main Street that day."

"I'm not nervous," she denied with a casual shrug. She knew she was a lousy liar, but she couldn't seem to help herself. It was a defensive maneuver straight out of the depths of her feminine psyche.

"Yeah, you are. You're trying to hide it, but you are. Do you think people are already talking about us behind our backs?"

"Of course not."

He took a step toward her and she automatically took a matching step back. "No social lies now, Carly," he warned her.

She could see amusement in his blue eyes. They also contained another more feral emotion that quickened her heartbeat and set her insides into a further quiver.

She shook her head. "I'm not lying," she replied evenly. She knew he was referring to her nervousness, but she was only answering the last question he had posed to her, the one about social lies.

"Well, then, if you're not lying and you're still nervous, the obvious conclusion is that it's men in general who upset your balance." He reached out to stroke her cheek. "And here I thought I was special."

Carly appreciated his drawing the wrong conclusion. It wasn't males in general who upset her equilibrium, not by a long shot. Only the ones who intimidated her sexually could throw her off balance, and Deke had pole-vaulted himself right back to the top of that list. It had been that way fifteen years ago; she had to face the fact that the passing of time hadn't changed things between them.

Deke had never been polite or predictable. Even as a teenager he had always seemed more grown-up than the other boys, probably because he always managed to do whatever he wanted. Following the logical conclusion to that line of thinking, she realized that Deke was right about Elvie. They were taking away his self-control even if the doctor and her mother thought it was the sensible thing to do.

"Don't worry, Carly," Deke interrupted her reverie. "One of the cardinal rules of life is 'Never fool around with your partner.' It takes your mind off the job at hand." His callused fingers brushed her skin again for a brief moment before he withdrew his hand, grinning at her as he arched his brows with good-natured lechery. "Then again, the only partner I ever had was a man, so I've never had to resist the temptation."

She stared at him a moment, then shook her head and laughed. This kind of teasing she could handle. "You and Elvie will probably be at each other's throats by the time we're finished with this thing. You of all people should know he's not the easiest person to get along with."

Deke grinned. "Yeah, I know it, all right. But what about you and me? Do you think we'll get along?"

"Why shouldn't we? We have the whole summer to get used to each other." Her smile faded. "Why did you come back to Justice, Deke? I would have thought it was the last place on earth you wanted to be."

"It is."

"So why did you come home? Are you getting tired of climbing mountains?"

He shrugged noncommittally. "Something like that. And by the way, I don't consider this place home anymore."

Carly's eyes flew to his face. She hadn't realized she'd said home. The word contained more than a hint of bitterness when it came from his lips. In some ways she knew what he was implying. When he was in high school he couldn't wait to get out, everyone in town knew that. It was probably the only thing she'd ever had in common with him. And yet, surprisingly enough, here he was, back in Justice to try to bring an old man's whim to fruition.

It must be a passing phase, she finally decided. Probably the result of too much altitude during his last trek up a mountain. Deke didn't have an altruistic bone in his body.

"What's it like, climbing a mountain?" she asked, suddenly very curious about the way Deke made a living.

"High up. Cold." He quickly changed the subject. "What's it like living in Paris?"

She smiled, her eyes shining. "Wonderful. I love everything about the culture and especially the way they preserve their history instead of trying to tear it down like we do. I suppose New York or Chicago have similar cultural attractions, but I guess I'm prejudiced because I feel the French are just so much more civilized. They seem to *savor* life. A lot of it has to do with the language. To me, French is like poetry and music combined. In any case, Justice is kind of a letdown after all that."

"Justice is a letdown after anything." He shook his head and shrugged. "It just depends on what you want out of life."

"Probably some of the same things you do. You're obviously searching for something more than provincial town life."

"Yeah, sure."

Deke fell silent after that. Carly wandered back to the couch, glancing over to find him staring down at his hands, lost in thought. "So," she said brightly, "do you know anything about Jesse James?"

"Not much. But it's not going to stop me from finding his loot."

"Did Elvie offer you a cut of whatever we find?"

If he noticed her sudden use of the plural pronoun, he didn't comment. "Sure. That's standard operating procedure. Elvie wouldn't expect a guy to do all that work without offering him some incentive."

"Of course not," she agreed, her brain sifting quickly through this new information. Some of the pieces were beginning to fall into place. "Well, as I said before, you can count me in."

"Good. Maybe you'll get lucky and we'll find there's something more to Elvie's map than wishful thinking."

"Maybe." She smiled at him. This treasure business wasn't such a bad idea, after all. Perhaps her unplanned sojourn in Justice would be one to remember.

Chapter Three

Elvie marched into the room holding up a dusty-looking brown book, obviously the diary he had talked about. Under his other arm he carried a battered shoe box which he set down on the coffee table.

"I got it," he shouted unnecessarily as he waved the book around.

Carly could see that the leather cover was water-stained. Mildew graced one corner; already the smell of it had reached where she was sitting, causing her to wrinkle her nose in distaste. Other spots, some ominously black and several a dusty white, spread in a marblelike design across the surface. Some intrepid soul had awkwardly mended the spine at one point, and the tape gaped like an open wound where it had lost its adhesive. She could still see areas of gold tooling that indicated what the book had looked like when it was new.

Her stomach dipped in excitement. "Can I see it, Uncle Elvie?" she asked, holding out her hand.

"Sure, niece. Just be careful, it's in a lot worse shape than the last time I looked at it."

"I will." She took the book gingerly from his grasp, laying it on her lap for a moment before she opened it. "Uncle Elvie? If we do find something, will it be ours or will it have to be turned over to the government or something?"

"The government!" Elvie snorted in disgust. "As long as the cave is on my land and I have this diary that proves that Jesse James intended it for my granddaddy, there won't be any question about turning it over to anybody."

She frowned. "But Jesse stole the stuff in the first place. Doesn't that still make it someone else's?"

"There's no way they can prove who he took it from, Carly," Deke said as he looked up from his perusal of the contents of the shoe box. "The main thing is that it's on somebody's property. You only have a problem when it's on land owned by the government or if it's under the ocean like all that Spanish gold that guy found off the coast of Florida."

"Oh." She carefully opened the diary to the first page. "Good, then let's get started."

"Wait a minute." Elvie held up his hands for attention. "Before we start I want to say something, just so everyone knows where they stand and there's no backstabbing or claim-jumping. We're going to divide whatever we find into thirds." He turned his attention to Carly. "I know my niece is wanting to fly back to Paris being as Missouri's not good enough for her."

"Uncle Elvie," she protested good-naturedly, "that's not the reason."

"No matter. This should allow you to go first class. And Deke—" he nodded at the younger man "—you'll probably just blow it on one of those high-stakes poker games you used to be so famous for, but you're welcome to it, anyway. The way I've got it figured, there should be enough to go around."

"Maybe we shouldn't count our chickens before they're hatched." Carly looked from one man to the other.

"Horse manure." Elvie snorted. "Now is exactly the right time to take care of details like this."

"You should take a larger cut, Elvie," Deke said, propping one booted foot on his knee as he sprawled comfortably in the chair. "After all, it's your map and your land."

Elvie rocked back and forth on his heels. "That's a fact. But the map's no good to me if I can't physically track down where that money is hidden. Which means I have two options." He ticked them off on his fingers. "One, I can hire some complete stranger to take care of this, someone I don't know from Adam, someone who isn't related to me or to anyone else I trust, or two, I can get you two young people to do it."

"All right, you win." Deke held up his hands in surrender. "You talked me into it."

"You'll take your third?"

Deke nodded. "I'll take my third."

Carly tried to keep the disgusted look off her face. She was sure that Deke had money stashed away. Mountain climbers were wined and dined by all kinds of geographic societies and fawned over by people with money who backed their expeditions. Weren't they?

"Well, I don't need more than the price of a plane ticket," she finally commented. "So if you need more money to get your farm up and running, you can have my share, too.''

"That's right kind of you, honey. I hope it won't be necessary.''

"How come you never looked for Jesse's stash before?'' she asked, idly turning over the pages of the diary.

"I never needed it before, Carly-girl. I had everything I ever wanted while I had the land and my freedom.''

"That must be a great way to live," Deke said, his comment sounding almost wistful.

"Yeah, buddy.'' Her uncle's face was alight with satisfaction and pride. "Now, lemme check the kitchen and see if there's any lemonade left. We need to celebrate.''

After he left the room, Carly glanced across to Deke. "I knew you weren't as altruistic as all that.''

He looked startled at her words. "I never said I was.''

"I thought you came back to Justice to help Elvie.''

"I did,'' he said in a silky voice. He uncrossed his legs and got up from his chair, quickly covering the small space between them.

She didn't back down. "It sure didn't take much persuading to get you to take your share.''

"I don't suppose it did.'' He leaned forward, grasping the arms of her chair, resting his weight on his hands until his face was only inches away from hers. "You think you've got me all figured out, don't you? The problem is, you don't know a damn thing about me.'' His hand lifted to grasp her chin in strong fingers, forcing her to meet his angry gaze. "You just think you do, along with everyone else in this town."

She opened her mouth to speak but couldn't think of a thing she wanted to say. He was overwhelming. She could smell the warm male scent of his skin, a mixture of the outdoors and the man himself. He didn't wear any after-shave. He didn't need anything to enhance the sheer masculine power he exuded as naturally as other people breathed.

He inched even closer, resting most of his weight on his one arm as he continued to hold her chin. His knees were pressing against hers; she had to make an effort to keep them clamped together since the weight of his solidly muscled body had her pinned against the cushions.

"The only person around here who didn't judge me was Elvie. Maybe that will help you to understand why I would do just about anything for the man even if you think I'm not noble enough to carry it through."

"That's not what I meant. I'm sorry," she whispered. "I thought mountain climbers made a lot of money."

Something flared in the depths of his eyes, but they kept unrelenting contact with hers. She couldn't look away even if she'd wanted to. But she certainly didn't want to.

He ignored her comment about mountain climbers to get right down to business. "How sorry?" he demanded bluntly, eyeing her mouth. His thumb brushed lightly along her lower lip.

"Not that sorry," she retorted quickly. Suddenly it seemed as though a freak force of nature had sucked all the air in the room out through the fireplace. She tried not to let him see the effect he was having on her, but she could tell that he knew exactly what he was doing to her equilibrium.

"Why not?"

She swallowed to moisten her dry throat. "Because . . . because one thing has nothing to do with the other. I only said I was sorry for judging you."

Although it seemed impossible to Carly, he moved still closer. Now he was only a lip length away from her mouth. She stopped breathing altogether for uncounted seconds before her lungs finally rebelled and she gasped a mouthful of air.

"A kiss is the universal medicine for whatever ails you," he explained, causing his breath to mingle with hers. His blue eyes glinted with teasing lights. "Didn't your mother ever kiss something better and didn't it always work?"

"A bruised ego is not exactly the same thing as a scraped knee," she told him, moving her head back the last small distance left. She pressed herself tightly against the headrest. If she tried to turn her head away now, she would have to meet Deke's lips on the way.

One glimpse at his face showed her that he was enjoying this. She could feel her cheeks reddening, and she hated herself for feeling so awkward. She was pretty good at handling men who were suave and subtle, but she was a little rusty with the kind who didn't play by the rules.

"Do I still make you nervous, Carly?" he asked in amusement, stroking her mouth with his thumb. He seemed fascinated with its texture, bringing in his fingers to help him sample it more thoroughly.

"My mother always told me that you were the kind of guy who would chase anything in skirts," she retorted.

"And you're afraid I'll chase you, is that it? But, Carly, you're not wearing a skirt."

She automatically looked down at her slacks, and when she glanced up again, his mouth was there to meet hers. His hand caressed her cheek as he angled his head to kiss her. His lips were warm and soft as they played over hers. His hand moved around to the back of her head, holding her in place so he could deepen the contact between them. She was helpless to do anything other than respond to him, the unique taste of his mouth, the musky male scent of his skin, the feel of his warm breath against her face.

And yet it was like no kiss she had ever experienced before. She didn't feel overwhelmed or imposed upon. She found herself raising her arms to entwine them around his neck, sinking her fingers into the thick hair at the nape, and pressing her body upward to garner as much contact with his body as she possibly could. She didn't recognize herself or her response, but she felt more reckless than she ever had in her entire life and she didn't care. She only knew she couldn't stop.

Oh, he was good, all right. Even with her limited experience, Carly knew that Deke was a skilled lover. By the time he finally broke away, she had learned the difference between a simple kiss and one that was a gourmet experience of the senses.

"Very nice," he said softly. "How about a hot summer affair?"

The soft giving mood he had coaxed from her shattered, and she pulled away from him. "No thanks. I'm going back to Paris, remember?"

"Yeah, but there's a lot of free-floating time before that happens." He frowned. "Do you have a boyfriend over there?"

"No," she admitted, then added, "not at the moment, anyway." She didn't want him to think she couldn't attract a Frenchman.

But that's not the trail his conjectures were traveling on, at all. "Frenchmen must be dumber than I figured."

"They are not!"

He laughed. "That was a compliment to you, *guapa*."

She eyed him warily. "What's *guapa?*"

"It means pretty one."

"Oh. I've heard that South American women are very beautiful."

"Some of them." He shrugged. "They're very good at making a man feel like a man. It's part of the entire machismo package you find at work down there."

"I suppose Frenchmen are like that, too. They make you feel very special. It may be a game, but I have to admit that it's very pleasant."

"Have you lost your taste for American men?" he asked. His joking tone belied the expression in his eyes, which was very intense.

She wanted to swallow, but she forced herself not to betray her awareness of the suddenly tense atmosphere that surrounded them. "I haven't seen any American men for over two years."

"That's not what I asked, but never mind." He stood up, shoving his hands into his pockets as he paced back across the room to his chair. "We need to concentrate on getting Elvie back on his feet by figuring out this map."

"Good idea."

They each settled down with the materials Elvie had given them. Carly began reading the diary while Deke perused the papers he'd been holding. Elvie came back with a big pitcher of lemonade, pouring for each of them, then toasting the enterprise by clinking glasses. Then he too made himself comfortable in his favorite chair with Jesse James's map and various intricately detailed land surveys from the government.

"This map supposedly shows the western edges of my property, but shoot fire, I can't figure out where this cave is supposed to be." Elvie ran his thumb along the line of his left suspender, tugging it away from his body as he frowned over the various papers spread across his lap. "Deke, come take a look."

Deke put the shoe box aside, coming to crouch next to the arm of Elvie's chair as he studied the maps. Carly could almost feel the intensity of his presence from across the room. He still retained the laid-back, unrushed quality of a Missouri man, but she felt it was only a veneer over the coiled inner spring of tension under the surface. This was not a man who would be happy doing things halfway.

"I don't know that area very well," Deke said slowly. He pointed to a series of parallel lines that indicated a depression of some sort running alongside the hill. "If we can find this, we should be able to follow it to the foot of this hill, here, where the cave is supposed to be. It looks like it could be an old, dried-up riverbed.

"Yeah, but the U.S. land survey map doesn't show it."

Deke frowned. "Maybe it's more of a gully. Maybe it's not as noticeable now as it was in Jesse's time." He looked at the date in the corner of the map. "This looks like the most recent survey of the area, and things can change in seventy-five years or so."

"You're probably right," the old man sighed.

"What about Artressa Brown?" Deke asked after a thoughtful pause. "She might know something about the area, especially if it involves Jesse James."

Carly smiled to herself as she waited for the explosion. She wasn't disappointed.

"That snake-eyed old biddy doesn't know anything about it! And I don't want her to, neither."

Deke backed off immediately. "Okay, okay. I just thought she might be able to help."

"She can't," Elvie grumbled half under his breath.

Carly grinned. She'd never actually met Artressa Brown, although obviously Deke knew something about her. She lived somewhere on the other side of Elvie's property, running a small all-purpose store by herself now that her husband had passed on. Carly thought she might have gone to school with Elvie, but she wasn't sure. All she knew was that her uncle had some kind of running feud with the woman and that he bristled every time her name was mentioned.

"Listen, tomorrow I'll take a ride out there and look around, see what I can find." Deke turned to Carly, who'd been watching the interaction with interest, her finger marking her place in the diary. "Find anything useful in there, Carly?"

"Not about Jesse James," she replied softly. "So far it's just been entries about farming, how many acres were going for cotton, how many for other crops, how many hands he was going to hire for the harvest." She blew out her breath. "I've still got over half the diary to go. What about those papers you were looking at?"

Deke shook his head. "Mostly old letters to relatives, a handful of flyers about the St. Louis world's fair of 1904, and advertisements for farming equipment. Interesting stuff, but nothing useful to us."

He jumped to his feet, his hands resting on the back of Elvie's chair. "How about if I leave you two to finish going through the paperwork here. With that map we've got enough to get started, and there are a lot of things I need to get done before we're ready to roll."

"That's fine with me," Carly said.

"I'm going to hit the road, then."

She stood up to escort him to the door. Elvie waved from his chair then went back to studying the maps.

Deke pushed open the front door then held it for her to follow, so she did. He walked down the porch stairs to his motorcycle, then he mounted the monstrous machine as easily as a cowboy might toss himself into the saddle. He beckoned for her to follow with a crooked finger.

She slowly approached him, eyeing the bike with some trepidation. A big cruiser like this one made her nervous simply because it belonged to Deke, and she didn't trust him not to give her a heart attack by peeling out of her driveway at ninety miles an hour in a cloud of gravel and dust.

She watched him put on his helmet. "I didn't think you'd wear one of those."

"Safety has to come first."

"What a sedate point of view, coming from you. Since when did you become worried about mundane concepts like safety?"

His grin was quick and easy. "There are some things that are givens in life, and wearing a helmet on a motorcycle is one of them. My head has been knocked around enough. Why don't you hop on? Just to try it out."

The bike was a huge Harley Davidson, obviously one of the newest models because it looked sleek and shiny and the gauges appeared state-of-the-art. There were three headlights in the front, making it look like a high-tech insect. The engine was a collection of metal shapes that reminded her of human insides spilling out in one of those horror movies.

She couldn't quite get her leg over the wide seat, so Deke helped haul her over. Her portion of the leather was slightly raised from where he sat and there were metal handrails for her to grip, although she had the feeling that they wouldn't be enough for her if Deke ever got up to any speed.

"Nice bike," she murmured.

"I'm glad you think so." He twisted around so he could look at her face. "If I'd known you could be won over so easily with a hot piece of machinery like this, I would have tried a little harder in high school."

"I doubt it," she countered dryly. "I was too young and innocent for you."

"Maybe. But your kiss was a revelation. It almost made me want to give up my wild ways."

She stared at him in amused disbelief as he buckled the strap underneath his chin then reached for his sunglasses.

"Don't give me that look," he said softly, one side of his mouth crooking up. "Didn't you know that the love of a good woman is supposed to tame even the wildest rebel?"

"That's what the old cliché says," she replied mildly. "Personally, I've never seen much evidence of it."

He grinned as he turned back around to start the engine. Carly was surprised to find that it didn't roar into life like most of the motorcycles she'd heard. It was more like a throaty purr that vibrated through every pore in her body and was oddly soothing to her nerves. He revved the throttle for a few moments. Carly decided it was time to get down before he really did take her for a ride. She scrambled to the ground.

"Goodbye, Deke."

"Adiós, guapa."

He shifted into gear and headed out the driveway, only fishtailing once as he turned onto the street. She knew it was a masterfully restrained performance.

CARLY DIDN'T SEE DEKE for three long, peaceful days. She should have known better than to think it could last. On the fourth, he rode up to the house, revving his engine a couple of times just to let her know he'd arrived. She put aside the fashion magazine she'd been looking at and headed for the door. Elvie must have heard the noise as well, because he was already there ahead of her, pushing open the screen door and stepping onto the porch.

"Deke looks like he's ready to get this show on the road," he told Carly over his shoulder.

She followed him outside. Her eyes widened in amazement as she saw the piles of equipment Deke had somehow managed to pack on the bike. As she watched, he removed the straps of a backpack from around his shoulders, swinging the entire contraption around to set it on the grass with ease. She stared at the other canvas bags Deke had neatly arranged on the back of the motorcycle and tied firmly in place against the metal backrest. A long metal pole poked out of one of them. Good luck to him if he planned to hike up into those mountains with all that gear, she thought.

He finally disentangled himself and strode over to them.

"You don't fool around when you wanna do something, do you, boy," Elvie said with a chortle. He sounded extremely pleased with the progress of his plans.

"The sooner we find this stash, the better off we'll all be," Deke replied, grinning.

He had on a T-shirt that he must have worn a thousand times before. The material was thin almost to the point of being see-through, and it hugged every rippling muscle as though Rodin had sculpted flesh and shirt together into one work of art. Carly tried not to stare. Looking at the French master's sensuous statues while she'd been in Paris had always aroused a thrill of decadent pleasure along her nerve endings, rather like the feeling she was experiencing now.

"Hi, Carly," he said, nodding in her direction, his eyes sparkling. She didn't trust that look.

"I thought you were going to go look around," she said politely.

"I did. I figure it won't take us longer than a week. Camping out in Missouri at this time of year will be a pleasure. There's not even any rain in the forecast for the next couple of days."

"How lovely."

He shrugged. "Yeah. My Mom said she'd come out here and stay with Elvie, so you won't have to worry about a thing. You'll be able to concentrate on the business at hand."

Her mouth dropped open. "No way!" She grabbed a handful of her hair, pushing it back from her face as she stared at him. "I'm not going camping with you."

"How else do you think we're going to locate that cave? You said you were in on this deal, you even shook hands on it. Now it's time to put your money where your mouth is."

Elvie immediately jumped in to add his opinion. "Carly, niece, you promised to help."

"I can't do it alone, Carly. I need you to come along with me. I've got extra gear for you, so all you have to do is grab a few clothes and we can get going."

"I agreed to help, but I didn't agree to lose the comforts of civilization for more than a morning or an afternoon," she muttered between clenched teeth. "I thought we would come home at the end of each day."

"Wastes too much time coming back."

"I hate camping."

"Of course you do," he agreed soothingly.

"I don't have anything to wear."

"Jeans will do just fine."

She looked across at her uncle, who was grinning like a fool, his eyes shining. He looked excited and so hopeful, like a small child about to receive the treat of a lifetime. He stood there in the driveway, his spine straight and unbent, his shoulders flung back as he fingered his suspenders in that habitual way of his. She knew there was no help for it now, the door of destiny had clanged shut behind her, and even though she had sworn to herself that she was absolutely tone-deaf when it came to the primitive call of the outdoors, she was about to embark on the camping trip of her life.

Events tumbled past in a blur after that. Somehow she stuffed some clothes and personal items into the backpack Deke handed her, thank goodness a smaller version of the one he proposed to carry. Elvie came into her room to hand her a framed picture of Jesse James to take along for inspiration, as well as the diary and the shoe box.

Shortly after that, Opal Baxter arrived, suitcase in hand. She was a small, neatly dressed woman who immediately moved into the kitchen and took up the task of washing the breakfast dishes. Deke loaded the gear into the small hatchback his mother had driven, and before she could say "This is a stickup" they were on their way, heading west toward the foothills of the Ozark Mountains.

"How come Uncle Elvie trusts you alone with me?" she finally asked him after several miles of scenery had glided by her passenger window. "If my mother knew, she would have a fit."

He laughed. "I don't know, I didn't ask him. Maybe it's because he knows you can't wait to get out of Justice." He downshifted as they hit a sharp curve in the road, then glanced over at her. "Or maybe he just figures if you haven't already succumbed to my notorious way with women, you must be immune."

She wasn't sure how to reply to that pronouncement, so she didn't.

"Don't worry," he continued cheerfully, "you should be safe enough. I haven't perfected my French accent quite yet. Or my French lovemaking technique. Besides, I'm not into all that fancy hand-kissing stuff. I happen to like the direct, all-American approach."

She gave him her best Gallic shrug. *"A chaqu'un son goût,"* she said with an airy wave of her hand. "To each his own."

They lapsed into silence after that exchange. As far as Carly was concerned there was nothing more to be said. He had coerced her into this expedition, but that didn't mean she had to like it. Actually, she didn't feel as angry as she thought she should be, but she figured she could at least keep up the pretense for a respectable length of time, just to soothe her feminine sense of propriety. She folded her arms and settled back into her seat, looking out the window at the rugged landscape.

It really was beautiful country here. She'd forgotten how appealing such natural landscapes could be, even though she now preferred the hedgerows, stone walls and fences that graced the countryside south of Paris. Still, there was something to be said for the untamed.

She glanced briefly at Deke, who remained absorbed in his own thoughts. She supposed she had to

include him in that category as well. He would be wild
and untamed with a woman. She could almost imagine the sexual energy he would generate in bed. She
just wasn't comfortable with men like that, probably
because they made no effort to put her at her ease. Her
thoughts immediately flashed to Jean-Claude Aragon, and she sighed.

He was the uncle of Claudine Fouget, one of her
classmates at the *école* in Paris where she'd spent her
junior year. Carly had never known anyone quite so
suave and sophisticated. He was the epitome of the
gallant Frenchman, and in her eyes, everything a man
should be. He was the one who had arranged a job for
her with Saronique, a small fashion design company
with a growing reputation for innovation. And
squeezed in between her long working hours he had
shown her his own special version of Paris, with many
of the tourist attractions as well as places no one but
the residents knew about.

She couldn't even imagine Deke acting the way
Jean-Claude did over a woman. A man like Deke had
a rough sort of charm, she supposed, but she imagined him to be the type who would expect a woman to
fall into bed with him whenever the urge hit him. Like
many American men, he wasn't comfortable talking
about real feelings and softer emotions like love and
tenderness.

She glanced over again, this time more assessingly.
He had one arm draped over the steering wheel in a
pose of complete authority over the car. His other
hand rested with quiet familiarity on the stick shift, the
way another man's hand might rest on a woman's
knee. She quickly squelched the curiosity she felt

about how he would behave if he was in love. Besides, he'd already told her how he liked it, direct and all-American, which wasn't the way her romantic soul envisioned intimacy with a man.

"Better hold on," he suddenly warned her just before he wrenched the wheel to the right, throwing them off the asphalt pavement and onto a crude dirt track.

Carly grabbed the door handle with one hand, using the other to brace herself against the dashboard as she bounced around the interior of the car like a marble in a pinball machine. When she glanced at Deke she could see that he was rolling with the rough motions of the car. He grinned when he saw the expression on her face.

"Don't fight it so hard and you won't get jerked around like that."

"Is that so?" she replied through clenched jaws. She could see that her discomfort amused him, but she didn't have time to get indignant over it. She was too busy trying to keep her teeth from grinding together and her neck from snapping.

He quirked his eyebrows at her. "How did someone who grew up in Justice ever become so citified?"

"I don't consider my reaction under these extreme circumstances *citified*," she retorted, sounding breathless because of the jerky movements of the car. "In my family, we only traveled on designated roadways. We didn't try to forge our own."

"Too bad. That means you never got yourself off the beaten track and into the unknown."

"You're the one who wanted me along," she said in self-defense, hating to talk because she knew she would end up chewing dirt for the rest of the day. "I never said I was very useful under these kinds of conditions.''

"I'll make sure you contribute your share, don't worry.''

Chapter Four

Maybe I don't want to contribute my fair share, she thought grimly to herself a couple of hours later as she struggled to keep pace with Deke's effortless strides. They were steadily climbing higher into the hills and she swore the air was thinner already.

She stifled a groan. Well, at least it wasn't Elvie whose leg muscles were burning and cramping and whose lungs were straining to suck in oxygen. The backpack seemed to grow heavier with each step. She wanted to appear sophisticated about this hiking business, but it wasn't easy trying to appear graceful and elegant while you were gasping for air as though you were about to collapse any minute. In any case, she didn't figure she was fooling Deke.

"Watch out for that rat snake on your left," he called back cheerfully over his shoulder.

Carly barely stifled the scream that came automatically to her lips at the thought of the slithery creature, even if it was harmless. She refused to give Deke the satisfaction of breaking into hysterics. He had to have known she was in no shape to go tramping through the Ozarks toting a twenty-pound load on her back. She was more the type to sit underneath a café awning with a cool drink in her hand. Maybe he thought he was taking it easy on her. He certainly seemed to have breath to spare since he was now whistling a jaunty tune. When he wasn't doing that he was pointing out the flora and fauna of the area as if she hadn't spent her entire life in Missouri.

"I hope you know where you're going," she said to his back. She knew she sounded testy but she couldn't help it. She had enough to cope with, and at this point she didn't have the energy to care what Deke thought.

"Not really," he replied with a nonchalant shrug.

The man was infuriating. Her feet were killing her in these skimpy tennis shoes, and here he was out on a summertime stroll! As Deke had so kindly explained earlier, he didn't want to take the time to break in a new pair of hiking boots for her. "Wear an extra pair of socks and you should be fine," he'd told her. Well, she didn't feel fine at all.

She scanned the horizon. "Why don't we stop and look at the map again."

"Don't need to. I have a good general idea of where we have to go, at least if that map is drawn to scale. We'll end up somewhere within the parameters of where I figure the cave is, give or take a mile."

I don't want to give a mile, she thought, gritting her teeth to keep back the retort. She hated to feel so grumpy and out of sorts, but when a woman felt as sweaty, tired and unglamorous as she did, it definitely tended to ruin her day.

"How soon till we get there?" she asked.

Deke actually stopped walking. He turned to look at her thoughtfully, his eyes alight with good humor.

"Probably in another hour or so. Let's take a short rest."

She knew he was stopping for her sake, but she was too grateful to argue. "Good idea," she said. She meant to ease herself down onto a nearby rock, but somehow, once she got going, she couldn't seem to stop her legs from buckling beneath her, and the momentum sent her crumbling into an undignified heap.

Deke sank to a graceful crouch in front of her. "You all right?"

"Perfectly."

"You look kind of flushed. You're not in very good shape, are you?"

She wanted to hit him over the head. "I'm a white-collar worker, not a member of a road construction crew."

"That's right, I forgot. You like Paris and culture and all that. You probably sip tea with your little finger in the air." He chuckled at the image.

"What an in-depth understanding you have of the subject," she retorted sweetly.

"Don't get your feathers all ruffled, Carly. I was only teasing. Are you always this grouchy?"

She sighed. "No." She struggled to her feet, then brushed off the back of her jeans, causing a small cloud of dust to fill the air. "Are you always this cheerful?"

He grinned. "We'll keep going until we reach that next ridge, and then we'll make camp for the night. It's getting close to sundown, anyway."

"Okay."

He thought he was doing her a favor. She didn't want to tell him that making camp was no better in her mind than hiking, so she said nothing as she followed him toward the brace of elm trees growing from the side of the ridge. She supposed it could have been worse; Deke might have brought horses. She definitely preferred her own limited power to a horse's.

Finally they stopped on the far side of a small meadow at the foot of the ridge Deke had pointed out. The wildflowers scattered throughout its grassy surface were quite pretty, and the mouthfuls of air she was surreptitiously dragging into her lungs were fresh and clean. Deke dropped his pack before clearing out a space for them. She watched him gather rocks and place them into a small circle for the fire. She wanted to offer to help, but he was working so efficiently and effortlessly that she decided that just this once she'd offer no comment. After all, he was the one who was experienced in the finer details of outdoor living.

After he had the fire going he reached into his pack and pulled out his sleeping bag, tossed it on the ground and threw himself down onto it. Then he rolled onto his side so he could look at her, his head pillowed in his hand. By this time she couldy hardly see his face against the backdrop of the rapidly darkening sky.

"Where's the tent?" she finally asked.

"Tent?" He sounded surprised.

"Yes, tent. You know, those little canvas contraptions that you get to sleep in when you're out in the wilderness."

"I didn't bring one."

"You mean you've been carrying that huge backpack around and it doesn't even have a tent in it? Where are we going to sleep?"

"In sleeping bags," he said. "On the ground. You don't need a tent at this time of the year, Carly. Besides, you'll miss gazing up at the Milky Way if you coop yourself up inside a tent."

"Of course." She hit her forehead with the palm of her hand, her tone sarcastic. "I wasn't thinking straight."

Deke ignored her comment. "Since I set up most of the camp, how about making dinner?"

She looked dubious. "Okay, but don't expect anything four-star."

He reached into his bag and pulled out a couple of cans of chili, a can opener and a rather battered-looking pot whose bottom was scorched from use. "I'm sure you wield a mean can opener. You can heat the chili in this." He handed her the items. "Just move that camp grate over the fire and set the pot on it."

"What about those rocks?" she asked anxiously. "Aren't they too close to the flames? When I was in the Girl Scouts, someone used the wrong kind and they actually exploded. I thought the marines had wandered down from the halls of Montezuma to shoot at us."

"Don't worry, they're fine." Deke chuckled. "I can see you've had some key experiences in the wilderness."

"Yeah." She struggled a minute with the opener but finally found that if she wrenched the handle with a certain downward motion the thing actually cut through the lid. "I got to help dig the latrine, which I thought was the most wretched experience on earth until we were all rudely awakened by Ginny Kitterman's screams. It seems she had fallen into the pit in the dark. I counted my blessings after that, believe me.''

"That's enough right there to put you off camping for life.''

She nodded. "Exactly.''

Deke lay there watching her clumsy efforts to open the second can, but he didn't offer to help her. Even in the deepening twilight, she could sense that he was assessing her; she could feel his hooded gaze skimming her face and hair with more than casual interest. She swallowed because her throat had tightened in quick reaction to his masculine curiosity. She could only assume it was idle, but she intended to make sure it stayed that way. As it was, just the thought of sleeping out in the middle of the Ozarks with wild animals creeping through the woods was almost enough to have her begging for sanctuary in his sleeping bag.

"So, what's on the agenda for tomorrow?'' she asked politely.

"We find the cave.''

"Just like that?''

"It shouldn't be too difficult.''

"Are you kidding? I saw that map. It didn't give any details, not a clue. The mountains depicted on that paper could be anywhere. We only have Uncle Elvie's word that it's these mountains.''

"We have more than that.'' He pulled out a piece of paper from his shirt pocket, handing it to her across the distance that separated them.

She reached for one of the flashlights lying on the ground, then opened the paper to find two neatly written paragraphs of directions. She began to read. "'Go to what is now called Ramsdell Creek. There is an old road or trail that leaves from the southwest corner and runs southwest. Follow this about two-and-a-half miles. You will come to a dim road running east and west. Go west on this road about two-thirds of a mile. . . .' Where did you get this?"

"From Elvie. He didn't want us to work too hard finding the cave."

"Did he have these directions all along?" she asked, the inflection in her voice rising on each syllable.

Deke shrugged casually. "I guess so."

"What happened to partners and handshakes and come hell or high water?"

"Maybe he wanted to surprise you."

She snorted. "I don't think so." She reached forward to give the chili a good shake, turning the pot around so the other side could warm up. Some of it splashed over the side to land in the fire with a sharp sizzling sound, but she ignored it. "I think he held that information back, as a kind of insurance policy until you could get here. If I had seen directions like those, I might have tried to find the cave myself, and he didn't think I could do it alone!"

"So?"

She chuckled sheepishly. "So, he was probably right. Although, you don't seem to be having any trouble. In fact, you make the task look as simple as baking a cake from a recipe."

"Hey, give me some credit. It wasn't all that simple," he protested with a grin. "After all, some of those roads and other landmarks that were mentioned are long gone."

"Whatever." She dismissed his troubles with an airy wave of her hand then frowned. "Then why was he so insistent on my coming along? You don't really need me. I can't even make a fire."

"Sure I do," he reassured her quickly. "For the company, if nothing else. Besides, you're his niece, his flesh and blood. You're representing him on this venture because he can't be here himself."

"I guess."

"Besides, he didn't want you to be too bored this summer after your exciting life in the big, bad city."

"He obviously doesn't know me very well if he thinks camping out is the proper antidote to boredom." She gazed at him, her expression alight with curiosity. "I suppose this is all pretty tame for you, though, after the kind of life you've been leading as a mountain climber."

"I wouldn't say that." Deke sat up with a forward rolling motion that brought him to his feet. "We need some more wood for the fire," he told her over his shoulder as he ambled toward the wooded area that marked the boundary of their camp. "There are a couple of plates and some silverware in my pack. Why don't you find them and start dishing up dinner."

"Okay."

He slipped into the dark woods, shaking his head at himself. Why didn't he just tell her the truth? He'd only written his mother a couple of times, but she must have read the damn letters to every gossip in town, since it seemed to be common knowledge that he climbed mountains for a living. His life was enough of a lie without adding another one to his credit.

As he began picking up stray branches and twigs, he cursed himself for being such a coward. Hell, it wasn't as if he was going to get anywhere with Carly. She wasn't the skinny little schoolgirl he had awed so easily with a motorcycle and a small-town, bad-boy reputation. This summer was just a stopover for her, a slight interruption in her plans, while for him it might mean the difference between continuing the course he was on or getting a fresh start on his life.

He thought over his interactions with Carly. He didn't consider himself vain—he knew he hadn't accomplished anything much in his life—but he couldn't remember meeting a woman who hadn't at least responded to his overtures, even if she chose not to take him up on it.

He realized that he had no idea how to be suave and sophisticated, how to woo her with poetic words and courtly gestures. In his mind it was a waste of time, but what the hell did he know? He was only a barbaric, uncouth American midwesterner who certainly hadn't gained any hot secrets while surviving in the backwaters of Peru.

He broke a large branch into several smaller pieces. He didn't need Carly Riddle, anyway. So what if she had the longest legs he had ever seen. So what if every night since he'd seen her again he had envisioned them wrapped around his waist, pulling him down into pleasurable oblivion. He should be glad she didn't realize the power she held over him, how vulnerable he was to her.

He wasn't stupid; he knew that she wanted someone who was his opposite in every way. If she responded to him, it would only be from the novelty of it, and he had no desire to provide her with a live sideshow. No, he chastised himself, it was better that she didn't reciprocate at all, and he'd better be damned careful to keep it light and friendly.

Carly heard his footsteps before she actually saw him. She turned back to the camp grate and scooped out the chili onto chipped blue enamel plates. When he sat down opposite her, she handed him the one she'd piled with the most food, along with a fork.

"I couldn't find any napkins," she told him in a soft voice.

"I'll just use my shirtsleeve," he muttered.

"What?"

"Nothing. I guess I forgot to pack the napkins, but there should be some paper towels in there somewhere."

She shrugged. "We can get by without them."

His eyes met hers across the fire. Carly was mesmerized by the repressed emotion she could see in their depths. She couldn't decipher the oddly intense mixture, but she realized that it now included anger and she wasn't about to provoke him by accidently saying the wrong thing if she could help it. After all, she was the novice; she would have to depend on him while they were out here in the middle of Elvie's land. She might be stubborn and opinionated, but she wasn't foolish.

"You were right, the stars sure are pretty," she said. "Will that fire keep away any animals that might come around?"

Deke's expression cleared as he chuckled. "You don't have to worry about that, Carly. They're as eager to avoid us as we are to avoid them. Besides, they don't like fire."

"That's good."

She chewed thoughtfully, her gaze off to the left of the crackling flames as she stared at the sky. Even though the valley they were in was already deeply immersed in dark, inky night, the last whisper of light was just disappearing below the far horizon to the west.

Carly gasped when she suddenly saw what appeared to be flashing lights. "What's that, a shooting star?"

"Where?"

"Right there," she pointed. "Just beyond the tree line on top of that hill."

They both stared for a moment, but that quadrant of the sky remained darkened, lit only by a lone, twinkling star.

"Tell me what you saw."

She considered for a moment. "Well, it was sort of like the spots you see after you get your picture taken with a flash camera. They danced along that ridge for a few seconds and then they were gone."

"Had you just looked at the fire?"

"No," she said, recalling her movements thoughtfully. "I'd been staring off in that direction for a while before it happened."

"Maybe you've just seen the dancing lights of the Ozarks."

"What're those?"

"I guess you know that there was a lot of silver around here at one time. The Spanish conquistadores used to mine it and then transport it through the mountains using mules. They'd take it to Mexico or Florida, and from there it would be shipped to Spain. Of course, the local Indians took exception to the disturbance of their ancient burial grounds. They would raid the mule caravans and kill any Spaniard they could find.

"Anyway, according to the old Indian legends, there are dancing lights anywhere there's gold or silver. They represent the spirits of the dead who guard such hidden riches and protect them from those who are unworthy."

"Oh." She set down her plate. "Is seeing them a good omen or a bad one?"

"I guess it depends on whether you're worthy or not." He pushed himself to his feet then went over to his pack and pulled out a coffeepot. "How about some coffee?"

"Sounds great."

He began preparing it, using water from one of the canteens. "Have you ever heard the legend about Arvil Crook's lost silver mine? It's supposed to be located somewhere around Justice."

"Arvil Crook." Carly's eyes widened in delight at the name. "I remember one of my teachers talking about him, way back in grammar school. But I don't recall anything more specific than that he was a pretty pathetic character."

"He sure was. Anyone who finds a mother lode of silver and thinks it's iron could justifiably be called pathetic."

"Is that what he did? Tell me, I don't remember anything about him finding silver."

Deke set the coffeepot on the grate before he began. "Arvil Crook was your typical subsistence farmer. He was poor and dirty and unkempt, according to his nearest neighbors, Tom and Lizzie Burke.

He had a wife, a poor, frail woman named Charleen, and a couple of kids. Anyway, Charleen was expecting. It was still winter and the crop had been pretty poor, so they were all half starving. Even though she'd already had two children, she was having a bad time with this one. Tom and Lizzie came over to help, but it was no use. The poor woman died and so did the baby.''

"Oh, how sad!''

"Yeah. Arvil appreciated Lizzie's help in easing his wife's last hours on earth. As a token of his gratitude, since he didn't have anything else to offer, he gave Tom a bag of bullets, telling him he'd found an old iron mine nearby and had fashioned them out of the ore he'd gotten there. In those days, bullets were hard to come by, so Tom was happy to accept them. It wasn't until several months later when he chipped a black spot off one of the bullets that he discovered they were fashioned out of pure silver.''

"Wow.''

"Naturally, Tom rushed right over to the Crook's farm, but the place was deserted. According to the blacksmith, Arvil had sent the boys on ahead to relatives in Texas, then packed up all his worldly goods so he could follow after them. He was never heard from again, and although Tom spent the rest of his life searching, he never found the mine, either.''

Carly bit her lip thoughtfully. "Where was the original Crook farm?''

"That's the thing—nobody's really sure. The Crooks were squatters, so they didn't have a legal claim to the land they were farming. Some people say it was right here around Justice, while others swear that the Crooks lived out closer to Poplar Bluff.''

''Those two places are more than a hundred miles apart.''

''Right. That's why no one knows where to search. Lizzie Burke sold the farm after Tom died. He had become totally obsessed with finding that mine and had just about ruined them in the process. She ended up in Kansas City where she peddled authentic maps purporting to lead to the lost silver mine. Trouble was, every few years the maps changed, until finally they had covered just about every area in the vicinity. She had that silver bullet, so people believed her and she made enough money to live out the rest of her life.''

''Why didn't someone just check the records to see where her farm had been?''

''They couldn't. The name Lizzie Burke wasn't her real one. She was using an alias.''

''My goodness. How come they never told us juicy details like that when I went to school?''

Deke shrugged. ''They probably thought it would warp your character. Mine was already beyond redemption.''

She shook her head in mock dismay. ''I'm sure that's what you always thought.''

''I didn't think it, I knew.''

She made a face. She wasn't about to argue with him about his character. ''Where's the ladies' room in this place? The one without the snakes.''

He laughed and pointed. ''Beyond that clump of trees should be safe enough, although I'm not making any money-back guarantees.''

''Thanks a lot.''

She made her way to the patch of ground indicated, making sure to keep the light of the campfire in the line of her peripheral vision. Thank goodness it was a mild summer evening; she had enough problems without worrying about the temperature.

When she returned she found that Deke had spread their sleeping bags on either side of the fire. Underneath hers he had thoughtfully spread a pad of some kind, and she smiled gratefully. She wasn't about to refuse even one extra inch of comfort between herself and that hard ground.

She wasn't sure whether she liked the idea of sleeping in the glow of the fire. She figured if she was illuminated by the firelight, any wayward animals who happened along would be able to see her.

And yet, the fire did give the illusion of safety, especially since she could see Deke across its golden light as he rummaged through his pack. She sat down on the edge of her sleeping bag, moving her own backpack so that it stood sentinel on the side that faced the dark. It wasn't the same as a locked door, but it was all there was.

"If you want, I could come and sleep by your side, Carly." His grin glinted in the light of the fire as he looked at her. "No extra charge."

"That's okay," she replied too quickly for the casual retort she intended it to be. "I'll manage."

"Still nervous?"

"I'm not used to sleeping outside."

"That's not what I meant and you know it. In spite of the low opinion you hold of me, I don't smoke, I don't cheat at cards and I don't try to charm every woman I meet into hopping in the sack with me."

"I can believe the part about not charming them," she said dryly, brushing the material along the top of the bag with idle fingers. "Seeing as how you have such a romantic way with words."

His eyes narrowed and his mouth tightened. "You don't like the thought of hopping in the sack? How would a man ask a woman to go to bed with him in French?"

"Well, *Voulez-vous coucher avec moi?* comes closest, I guess."

"And that means, Will you go to bed with me?"

She nodded.

"How would you say, 'I want to make love with you'?"

She swallowed as she felt the heat rising up her neck to flood her face. Other parts of her body felt flushed, as well.

"Um . . . *Je veux faire l'amour avec toi.*"

He repeated the phrase after her, his voice caressing the syllables in a way she chose to ignore. Her own peace of mind was at stake here, not to mention her pride.

"You have a good ear for languages," she told him. "Most people wouldn't be able to get past the first three words on their initial try. But of course, you probably speak Spanish, don't you?"

"Enough to get by."

His eyes met hers, and her stomach clenched for a moment before the blood began throbbing through her veins. She couldn't think of anything else to do so she crawled into her sleeping bag.

"You gonna sleep with all your clothes on?" he asked. The firelight highlighted the glint of amusement that was never absent from his eyes when he pointed out her lack of camping skills. "You should at least take your jeans off. They tend to restrict the circulation."

Her circulation was pumping along just fine at the moment. "Thanks, I will."

"How are you going to do that when you're already inside the sleeping bag?"

"Don't worry, I'll manage."

"Okay." He stood up and shrugged out of his T-shirt. His torso gleamed the most beautiful bronze as the fire cast intriguing shadows along the sleek curves of his muscles. "I once saw a woman put on a nightgown over the top of her clothes," he told her conversationally as he reached down to unsnap his jeans. "Then she took off her blouse and bra and everything else that was underneath the gown, and would you believe she did it without even showing a flash of skin?"

The sound of his zipper seemed unnaturally loud, but Carly couldn't quite look away. The material of his jeans was so well-fitted to his body that it seemed to cling there lovingly. Dangerously. And still she stared. Deke wouldn't be doing this if he didn't want her to look, she assured her guilty conscience.

"Men don't do it like that," he told her, his hands going to his hips to pull down the pants.

He stopped right there, but she didn't see because she quickly averted her eyes. Even in the dim light he could tell that her blush deepened and he sighed. She was making him crazy all right, driving him to pull a stunt like this, just to make her aware of him as a man and not the uncouth renegade he was in high school.

Hadn't he already come to a decision about this? What the hell was he doing, anyway, trying to get close to her when all she had on her mind was an unobtainable storybook romance with some perfect French Sir Lancelot.

He quickly doffed his jeans, leaving on his underwear for the sake of her modesty, and slid into the sleeping bag. "It's safe, you can look now," he said dryly.

He glanced over to see Carly's sleeping bag moving around on the grassy slope. She was obviously squirming around inside, taking off her jeans. He chuckled. He knew it was a simple-enough matter to take them off while inside a sleeping bag, but he wondered how she was going to get them back on in the morning.

"Good night," he called.

"Good night."

He lay back, resting his head on his arms as he stared at the sky. A shooting star flashed across his line of vision, burning out so quickly he almost doubted that he had actually seen it. If he were a romantic kind of guy he would point it out to Carly and tell her to make a wish on it.

Romance, hah. He had never really understood the concept. There was sex and there was love, but he couldn't fathom this thing called romance. Hearts and flowers and ornate language were all very nice, but they avoided the real issues that always cropped up when men and women got together. And yet as phony as that kind of behavior appeared to him from his male perspective, he realized that women seemed to like it and the men who provided them with it.

He hadn't been kidding her when he said he liked it direct. He wasn't a frilly kind of guy. Why couldn't women be as uncomplicated? Why couldn't they just say whether they wanted you or not? Why was it so insulting to a woman when a man said he wanted to sleep with her? Was it so wrong to want to be close to someone, even if it didn't end up lasting forever?

He sighed. Maybe he should just ask Carly outright if she was interested. He'd sort of done that in Elvie's living room the other day when he'd asked her for a summer fling. Now that he considered it, that had been a bad move. He was arbitrarily putting a cap on their time together, and most women craved those undying words of love, even if both of you knew it wasn't going to last. The only thing he could say in his defense was that he knew she was leaving and that he was logically incorporating that knowledge into his pitch.

He shifted onto his side. What was he supposed to do with the feelings she had aroused in him? Somehow, because she wanted so badly to leave, he found himself experiencing crazy flashes of wanting to stay, to settle down and plant some roots. He'd never been happy hanging around in one spot—maybe he was getting his mid-life crisis early.

He glanced across the flickering flames of the fire. All was quiet and still. Carly must be sleeping. He wanted to get up and check on her, but he knew if she was awake and saw him looming over her in his underwear she would think he was trying to hop in the sack with her. Although he could think of nothing better, he wasn't about to try anything like that without an invitation. And just maybe he'd get one before this adventure ended.

Chapter Five

Carly awoke the next morning to the welcome aroma of coffee. When she opened her eyes, she found herself staring directly at Deke, who was gazing back at her. Night's chill still hung in the air, and he had on a flannel shirt for warmth.

"Good morning." She smiled. Who would have ever believed she could sleep so deeply and dreamlessly throughout a night spent in the bosom of Mother Nature, she reflected sleepily as she rubbed her eyes and brushed the hair back from her face in a single motion. Somehow, being with Deke, she had felt safe and protected. And why not, she decided in good-natured self-defense. Camping out like this was probably tame stuff compared to the adventures he'd had along the way.

"Good morning," he returned. He was grinning widely, obviously in good humor as he held up the pot. "How about some coffee?"

"Please." She sat up, her bone-cracking stretches and yawns causing the sleeping bag to fall down around her waist. Although she had worn a long-sleeved shirt to sleep in, the air was already producing a healthy case of goose bumps along her arms and legs. She reached out for her sweater, suddenly realizing that the lower half of her body was clad only in panties and that she would have to figure out a modest way to put her jeans back on.

Deke handed her a steaming cup of coffee, and she gratefully took a sip, assessing the situation. It looked as though Deke had been up for quite a while, which probably meant that he was anxious to get going. Furthermore, he also probably had nothing better to do than to sit and wait, watching her the entire time.

"Here, have a doughnut." He handed her a stiff plastic tray that held a dozen of the powdered sugar variety. "Sorry, no croissants."

She smiled at his funny French accent, raising her eyebrows at him as she bit into her breakfast. He must be in a good mood if he could make jokes. She couldn't exactly say the same thing about herself, not when she was longing for a good hot shower. "That's okay, these are fine."

"I got you some water from that creek we passed so you can wash up if you like. I'm going to go scout up ahead for a bit."

"Thank you." She felt a rush of warmth at his thoughtfulness. Maybe there was some hope for him yet.

After he left, she quickly slipped into her jeans, then took care of all her morning ablutions as best she could under the primitive circumstances. She had to admit that the air smelled exceptionally crisp and clean and the sound of birds that drifted on the soft breeze, without the noise of automobiles to cloak it, was delightful. Now, if she had one of those camper vehicles with a bathroom in it and a softer bed, she would think she'd gone straight to heaven. Stretching her stiff muscles with a groan, she began to tidy up around the campsite.

Deke returned from his foray looking as cheerful as when he had left. "We're definitely on the right track. Those directions are pretty explicit."

They left their packs neatly stashed under a tree, taking only a few essentials with them. "If I'm correct about this, the cave should be fairly close by," Deke explained. His voice reflected some of the excitement that was beginning to stir in her, and his blue eyes sparkled. She had to admit he looked quite appealing at this early hour of the morning.

After ten minutes of steady climbing, they reached a particularly steep, rocky incline. Deke halted abruptly, putting out a hand to steady her. She stared at the angled hillside, wondering what it indicated.

"This is it," Deke announced. He folded up the maps and stuffed them inside his shirt.

"This?" Carly was dumbfounded. "I don't see anything. Are you telling me that there's a cave entrance somewhere along the face of that cliff?"

"It's hardly a cliff, Carly, but yes, according to these directions, we have arrived. The entrance is probably pretty well hidden, otherwise someone else would have stumbled across it before now. Why don't you wait here."

"Brilliant idea." She walked over to a large rock, brushed off its surface, then gingerly sat down.

She spent the rest of the morning scanning the hillside for an opening. Even with binoculars she wasn't having any success. Yards above her, Deke clung to the rocks and scrub, systematically searching for the cave. Feeling utterly useless, but unable to just sit there idly, she did the best she could, even going so far as to search the lower regions that she could reach by foot.

Sometime just before noon he gave a shout. "I've found it."

As she looked up, he disappeared into the cliff. Even though she had seen him go into an opening, she lost the spot as soon as he entered it. She waited for what seemed like an eternity before he reappeared.

"Now what?" she shouted up to him.

He came sliding down the hill, bringing an avalanche of rocks and dirt with him until he landed at her feet. His face was roguishly dirty and streaked with sweat, but he was grinning widely. "First we eat something for lunch and then we go exploring."

He had packed some sandwiches, and they sat in the shade of a large elm tree to eat them. Although they were slightly stale after a day in the backpack, Carly thought she had never tasted anything so good. Hunger was definitely the best seasoning. She glanced over at Deke. He was lying on the ground looking as comfortable as a cat. She couldn't help noticing his strong white teeth. His lips were well-defined and more than a little sexy if you were attracted to the rugged outdoors kind of man.

But he'd made absolutely no concessions to fashion, she reflected, surreptitiously sizing him up. She tried to picture Jean-Claude Aragon wearing clothes like Deke's but it was an impossible task. Jean-Claude's jeans were casual but he combined them with beautiful shirts and sweaters that emphasized his Gallic good looks in a way Deke could never manage.

Jean-Claude also sported a very masculine watch on his wrist and an expensive topaz ring.

Still, she couldn't help the small tug of curiosity that nibbled at the edges of her thoughts. It was a little exciting to think of having all that pure masculinity to herself, to be able to stroke that skin and caress those muscles, to kiss those lips and have those strong teeth nibble on her ear. She quickly snapped her attention back to her food. Enough of that. Idle curiosity might become a dangerous thing if she wasn't careful.

She finished the last bite, then looked thoughtfully at the hillside. "How am I going to get up there?"

"I'll help you. It's not as bad as it looks."

She made a face. "If you say so."

He grabbed her hand and pulled her to her feet. Then he picked up his pack, tossed its strap over his shoulder and beckoned her to follow him.

The first part of the climb was easy. They reached the lower ledge in minutes, and Carly was proud to find that she wasn't even out of breath. But as she gazed up at the sharp incline that awaited them, she realized she wouldn't be able to make that claim for much longer.

She started when she felt Deke reach around her waist. He was tying a rope there and attaching the other end to his belt. "I don't want you to fall. It's only a short climb, but this way I can keep you from sliding back down the side of that escarpment."

"A noble enterprise," she said with a smile. "I appreciate it." She wasn't too proud to admit that she knew nothing about climbing ninety-degree inclines.

"Come on."

In the end it wasn't half as bad as she had anticipated as long as she didn't think about the return trip down the side of the hill. She only lost her footing once, and then Deke's rope had instantly provided the support and traction she needed to pull herself back in line.

She looked up to find Deke clinging to the small outcropping of rock outside the cave entrance. "Here," he said, maneuvering her into place in front of him. "You go in first. Just watch your head when you get inside and wait for me."

"Okay."

She scrambled through the slit, trying not to think about the tons of dirt and rock that lay above her and that might come crashing down on her head at any moment. For a brief instant she felt a terrible fear as the walls squeezed her body, leaving her barely enough room to crawl. Then suddenly she pushed through to a small opening, like a room.

Seconds later Deke was with her and she found herself giggling in relief. The noise sounded eerie in the small contained space, so she stopped. "I sound like a madwoman."

"These caverns have a way of distorting sound," he told her. He had switched on his flashlight even though light filtered in from outside. He swung the strong, steady beam around the perimeters of the small cave that they found themselves in. Actually, it was more like an animal's lair than a bona fide cave. There was hardly enough room to stand. But then, Deke's light caught the disappearing recess of another tunnel in one corner.

"Come over here."

He tugged her toward him and began to untie the rope. She didn't mean to, but she couldn't help avoiding his gaze. What made her even more nervous was the fact that he never stopped watching her, untying the rope by feel without moving his gaze from hers. She found herself wishing that his hands would slide higher until they touched her breasts, and just the thought set her heart pounding in excitement. Being in the wilderness must bring out the baser instincts, she thought to herself.

"Why won't you look at me?" he asked quietly.

She was embarrassed that he had brought up the subject head on, and even more uncomfortable with the lascivious nature of her thoughts. She only hoped he hadn't seen that brief moment of soft yearning in her expression. He didn't mince words or play social games, and because of that she found him hard to answer, even if it was becoming easier to trust him.

She shrugged, not knowing what to say.

"Look at me, *guapa*," he urged her, using his fingers to gently turn her head so that she was forced to either close her eyes or gaze directly into his. It was less embarrassing to look. "Let's clear the air, okay?"

She nodded weakly. It was much too intimate being in this small space with him, especially since both of them knew there wasn't another human being around for miles.

"We're really going to have to work together from now on. It's important that we be attuned to each other." He watched her intently, his face close to hers.

"What do you mean?"

"I mean this electromagnetic force field that's between us, this tension and the awareness that goes along with it. I don't know whether it's good or bad." He lifted his hand to touch her cheek and she drew in a quick breath.

"See, that's what I mean." He coiled the rope and set it to one side. "Look, Carly, when you have a partner in something like this, you have to trust each other. Nature is totally unforgiving, she can crush puny human presumptions in a split second. Now, it's not that I think being in this cave is as dangerous as something like skydiving, but it doesn't hurt to cover all the bases."

"Of course." She nodded, trying to appear serious but unconcerned.

He glanced at her expression. "Look, I've never been in a situation like this with a woman. If you were a guy, I'd know what to expect from you and I could treat you in a certain way. Guys are up front."

He paused, blowing out his breath with a frustrated hiss. "I'd better just say it. It seems to be my damned problem, anyway. I just want to clear the air about how you make me feel. I thought maybe if I simply told you that I've been wanting to get inside your sleeping bag and we both knew it instead of just me knowing, then we could get on with looking for the treasure in an orderly fashion." His eyes met hers, and she felt an electric jolt of awareness arc between them. "So now I've told you. Okay?"

"Uh...sure," she managed to mumble in reply. Her brain had decided to shut down operations. It didn't like the confusion factor.

"Good." His thumb caressed her cheek, lingering there for a heart-stopping moment before he reluctantly moved it away. His smile was forced, almost as though his back teeth were clenched together. He looked more like a man in pain than one locked in the throes of desire. "Just give me a minute to get set up here and then we'll head down that passage."

Carly nodded as she sat there on the dirty floor of the cave. She was shocked. No, she was totally stunned. As if complete paralysis of emotions wasn't jarring enough, she was also experiencing an odd mixture of pride and excitement. It wasn't every day that a man told her he wanted to make love to her, even if the words he'd used were less than poetic. She didn't know what to say. Deke wanted her, but he seemed to be dealing with it in a rational fashion that irked her the more she considered it. Oh yes, he said he wanted her, but then he turned around to nicely explain how it was interfering with the expedition and that he needed to clear the air. Well, maybe she didn't like the idea that she could be brushed away with a few simple statements of fact and a cheerful "let's carry on."

What kind of five-and-dime-store brand of desire was this? Passion should be out of control, burning, flaming, a conflagration of the senses. She frowned. Maybe she just didn't inspire that kind of passion in a man. Could that be the reason she wanted a Frenchman so much, the fact that Frenchmen were so good with words and so able to make a woman feel like the most desirable creature in the world with just a gesture and a glance. A Frenchman certainly wouldn't bluntly state that he wanted to crawl into her sleeping bag with her. And he wouldn't drag her through a dark, dirty cave, either.

A sharp, banging noise jerked Carly from her angry contemplations. Deke was hammering a metal eyelet into the stone wall, just before the tunnel entrance. He had a ball of heavy cord attached to his waist, and he soon had the end of it tied securely to the metal ring.

"Just like Hansel and Gretel," he told her.

"They left a trail of crumbs."

Deke answered her with a shrug. He seemed cheerful now that he had gotten everything off his chest. "Well, the idea is similar. We're going to use this simple but effective system to make sure we can find our way back. Especially since I have no idea how big or how complex this cave system is." He paused at the tunnel's entrance. "Why don't you put on your flashlight, too."

She made a face at his back before struggling on her hands and knees behind him as he crawled easily ahead. "I think I would have been better off with one of those miner's hats that have the light already built in. I seem to need the use of both my hands."

"Okay, never mind the extra light. We don't really need it right now. I just thought you might feel better being in control of your own source of light. It's going to get mighty dark in there once we leave this area."

"Don't worry about me, I'll be fine," she said. She tucked the flashlight into her jeans and crawled after him.

They didn't talk much for a while. She figured Deke was concentrating on the business at hand, but the reason for her silence was more pragmatic. She didn't want him to know how short of breath she was both from her exertions and from the pressing blackness just outside the beam of Deke's light. She tried to rationalize her fears by telling herself that the air in the passage was fetid and hard to breathe, but she had to admit it felt quite fresh against her face.

Suddenly Deke disappeared from sight. She found out why when she followed him around a sharp corner and into a huge, lofty cavern. His light didn't even penetrate enough of the darkness to reach the ceiling. She quickly stood up and grabbed for her own flashlight, flicking it on and adding its strength to his as he pointed it around the room.

"Oh my goodness," she exclaimed.

"Incredible," Deke echoed her sentiment.

"It's like one of the natural wonders of the world," she said. Her voice disappeared into the vastness of the room. "I've never seen anything like it."

They shone their lights around the perimeters of the cavern. A rainbow of colors was reflected back at them. On one side, the walls were smooth and shiny, as though water had softly eroded them until every sharp edge had been blunted into the smooth, almost seamless beauty before them. Over on the far side of the hexagonal-shaped room, there seemed to be a couple of tunnels leading off into the unfathomable dark beyond. Even when Carly flashed her light into each gaping entrance, she could barely see more than a few feet beyond the portals. Oddly enough there wasn't much dirt on the floor in this area. The air was cool and moist and seemed to be an even temperature, which she guessed to be somewhere around fifty degrees.

"It's like being in church," Carly said in a whisper. She was in awe.

"It does have a sort of holiness about it, doesn't it? But then I've always found the natural world more impressive than anything man could ever make."

Carly knew it was a small dig at her appreciation of art and music and literature, but since she really couldn't disagree with him at this moment, she didn't say anything. Besides, how many people got to see something like this?

"Well, what now?" she asked.

"Let's try one of those tunnels and see where it takes us."

Deke quickly hammered in another eyelet while Carly continued to look around the room. Her flashlight caught some writing on the wall and she gasped, moving closer so she could inspect it more thoroughly.

"Look, Deke."

There on the wall about eye level was a signature written in what looked like faint ink: "Beach and Steel, Explorers, 1837."

"Looks like someone was here before us," Deke said. He ran his fingers over the inscription. "I think they might have signed their names in some kind of berry juice."

"Yes, it does have a rusty-looking cast to it," she agreed with a grin. "Unless it's blood." She passed the beam of light in careful arcs up and down the wall, but couldn't find any other writing. "Surely they weren't the only ones who came through here."

"It's hard to say. I've been in some caves that had so many names and dates filling the walls they looked like the subway in New York City." He paused thoughtfully. "There have been some earthquakes in these parts. I have a hunch that's how the entrance to this place ended up where it is and only Elvie's map reflects the new entrance."

"Then that means maybe no one has found Jesse's hidden stash."

"There's a good possibility." He smiled at her. "Catching, isn't it?"

"You mean treasure fever?"

"Sure." He grinned. "In spite of the camping and the dirt and the lack of civilized culture, you seem to be doing all right."

"So, I'm not immune. Did you think I would be?"

"Nope. I'm glad to see what's under the veneer."

"It's not veneer. You make me sound like a piece of cheap furniture. We all have our likes and dislikes, and I'm no different from anyone else in that respect."

"You sure made it sound like there wasn't anything outside of Paris that was worth spit."

She rolled her eyes. "Well, I didn't mean to. I realize that other people have valid opinions."

"Glad to hear it."

She smiled thoughtfully. Of course, he would never get her to agree totally with his principles and priorities, just as she realized he would never totally agree with hers. As far as she was concerned, that's what made the world go round. The only explanation she could find for the sudden and compelling urge she felt to meet him in the middle was that women were just too accommodating for their own good. He wasn't asking her to compromise and she wasn't about to, she stoutly assured herself.

Deke attached the twine to the metal ring before beckoning her to follow him. Carly swallowed hard as her stomach dipped in excitement and nodded.

Hours later, they were still roaming up and down an endless array of tunnels. She thought they must have traveled enough miles in this underground labyrinth to have reached Kansas. Some of the passages were wide, some narrow, some plain and some filled with incredible beauty. One they'd stumbled upon had a small grottolike spring with a latticework of glittering crystals that put diamonds to shame. She was sure they had crisscrossed over their own trail, but Deke assured her they hadn't passed the length of twine. They also hadn't seen any sign of the bank money.

"Maybe it's on some ledge like that one above us," Carly said to Deke's back as she followed him down yet another winding tunnel. "Maybe he sank it in that spring, in a plastic bag or whatever the nineteenth-century equivalent would be."

Deke shook his head. "I don't know, Carly. I do know that we're going nowhere fast just wandering around like this."

"Didn't Elvie give you the written directions for the cave as well?" she asked sweetly. "He seems to have clued you in on everything else."

"I wish he had. I never thought the cave would be a maze like this."

"Personally I'm starting to feel like one of those rats they use in scientific experiments." She kicked a rock out of her way with a satisfying thunk.

"Yeah, then where's the reward?"

"You only get the reward if you take the right path," she replied gloomily. "I guess we flunked. Can we rest for a while?"

"Best not to. We need to be on our way out of here. It's going to be getting dark outside soon."

They followed the cord, tracking back down endless corridors until finally they were in the large main cavern. Carly realized again how small and insignificant the two of them were in the face of such a natural wonder. Then again, she had felt the same way inside Notre Dame cathedral, walking down the nave as the afternoon sunlight filtered in through the stained glass windows high above her head. Of course, it had taken man a few hundred years to complete the cathedral, while she supposed Mother Nature could form a cavern like this with one earthquake. Still, the tunnels probably needed thousands of years of water erosion to attain their present configuration.

She breathed in the cool, moist air, feeling its clammy caress on her arms and face. At least she could appreciate both kinds of achievement, unlike other hardheaded individuals. She glanced at Deke, who was busy securing the cord to the eyelet. The irregular illumination provided by their flashlights had an odd effect on the planes of his face, but he still looked strikingly handsome. He turned toward her, causing the light to exaggerate the stubborn set of his jaw until he looked almost like a caricature, reminiscent of some cartoon hero.

"I hope you brought a lot of that twine with you," she commented, wondering which would give out first, her or the cord.

He chuckled. "Don't worry, I have enough to keep us busy for a long while."

She emerged from the cavern after Deke to find that he was right about the time of day; the sun was already low on the western horizon. They barely had enough light to make it back to camp. This time, Carly helped set up the sleeping bags, although she still left the fire to Deke.

"What's for dinner?" she asked. Between all the exercise and fresh air, she found that her appetite had increased enormously.

"Stew," was the laconic reply.

Carly giggled to herself. Canned stew sounded like heaven. At this point she probably could have chewed on that awful beef jerky and enjoyed it. "Are you cooking?"

"Sure."

She sat down on her sleeping bag, curling her legs to one side and simply absorbing the sounds and smells of the evening. It was quite lovely here on the side of the hill. Frogs were just beginning to croak and hum in the distance somewhere, and the drone of crickets and cicadas added a higher-pitched counterpoint. Across the now-crackling fire, Deke sat down on his sleeping bag, tending to dinner.

"What if we don't find anything tomorrow?"

He sighed, his gaze lifting to meet hers. Once again she felt that sudden shock of excitement and connection that she'd experienced before. It was almost as though they were two charged particles who could never come close together without generating electricity. And yet it had an element of recognition, as though she had always been waiting for just this reaction and had only now just discovered it. But that was nonsense, of course.

She was probably just ripe for dalliance, the victim of a head stuffed with visions of romantic encounters in foreign places, and she considered this uninhabited backwoods a foreign place. Besides, she reminded herself, it was summer, and that particular time of the year seemed to call forth longings and urges that everyone knew lay dormant in the cold winter months. Deke probably felt the same urges for the same reasons. It was nothing to worry about.

"If we don't find anything by lunchtime, we'd better go back to the drawing board," he said, breaking into her thoughts.

"That sounds like a great idea, but how do we do that?"

"We go through that diary again with a fine-tooth comb."

"I've already been through it three times, but you're welcome to try. Maybe you'll see something in there that I couldn't."

"In any case, I'm not giving up." He rubbed his neck.

"Me, neither." She laughed, surprised at her own vehemence and at her desire for more of this torture. She had to admit she was starting to have fun; she hadn't realized that after a while the physical discomfort of the trail would fade into the background and leave her mind and senses free to enjoy other things.

Deke stared at Carly, amazed at the change she had undergone in just a few short days away from what she liked to call civilization. Her face was lightly tanned and she seemed to glow from the inside. He found that

he was not only searching for the treasure to help Elvie get his farm back and to obtain money for a new
start, he was also doing it for Carly. He wanted her to
have her plane ticket to Paris if that's what her heart
truly desired. If anyone understood about dreams, he
did. Even if his had gone by the wayside he could insure that the people he cared about had theirs.

"There must be some kind of map to that cave," he
said aloud, his voice fierce. "The odds of finding the
right tunnel just by blundering around in there are
pretty slim."

"Let's see how we do in the morning."

He handed her a plate of steaming stew.

"Mmm. Smells good," she said.

"Yeah. The secret's in the wrist and how you shift
the stuff around in the pot."

"What's it like in South America?" she asked
softly. She blew on a forkful of stew before carefully
sliding it into her mouth.

Deke shook his head, his expression intense. "I
spent most of my time in Peru. The country there is
spectacular, but rugged and unforgiving. You can go
from seaside to desert to jungle to mountains in the
course of a single day.

Her smile was warm, her face alight with interest.
He felt very close to her in that moment, a new and
scary sensation that left him feeling exposed and vulnerable. And yet he wasn't ready to cut it off.

"It sounds beautiful," she said.

"It is, but the system of government is pretty
screwed up. There's a lot of poverty, but the people are
very proud. Many of them follow the old Inca ways,
especially in the mountains. They only ask to be left

alone to live their lives, but certain political fanatics have other ideas.

"I know this boy there, Esteban. The poor kid had to flee from the countryside after his parents were murdered by Shining Path terrorists for refusing to turn him over for training as a member." He gritted his teeth. "Nine years old and they wanted him to carry a gun.

"I first noticed him begging from a couple of American tourists. The man hadn't realized that the kid had picked his pockets clean before he had even turned away. Anyway, I made him give the wallet back, and I got him a job running errands for an American friend of mine who has a transport business there."

Even without closing his eyes Deke could still visualize Esteban's eager expression as he had followed Deke around Santa Rosaria, pointing out the sights, warning him of people and places to avoid.

"That poor child," Carly whispered in horror. He thought he detected the sheen of tears in her eyes.

He shrugged. "My partner, Bill, is looking after him. I also left some money with the Sisters of Mercy just in case Bill takes off for a week on a delivery."

"That was kind of you."

"Kind of me? No, you don't know what you're talking about."

He threw his plate aside then reached for his backpack, extracting the coffeepot. He began to measure the grounds into it with quick, jerky motions. Carly remained silent. It was obvious she didn't know what to say to his outburst, and he couldn't blame her.

"Listen, you don't need to hear about any of this. It's in the past, over and done with." He shoved the coffeepot down on the grate over the fire.

"Obviously you don't think it's over and done with."

"It doesn't matter what I think. That's just the way things are."

She stared at him, looking unconvinced.

"You think I'm running away from something, don't you? What about you, Miss Carly Riddle? If you're able to handle things so well, how come you're so hot to get away from here? Aren't you running away from something, too?"

"Wanting a career in Paris is not the same thing at all."

"Isn't it?"

"Of course not."

"Have you ever thought that maybe you're avoiding looking too closely at yourself?"

Their gazes snagged and held. "I am not avoiding anything," she said in hot denial. "Where do you come up with these weird ideas?"

He kept staring at her. "You're avoiding this thing that's sprung up between us. You probably think it's just sex, but it could turn into something more."

"That's a laugh. You're the first one who would grab the sex and run before it ever had the chance to turn into something more."

"There you go again, judging my character without knowing what you're talking about. I'm getting tired of it." He rose to his feet then crossed the small distance between them. "I repeat, you didn't know me in high school and you don't know me now."

Carly stared straight ahead. She knew he was looming over her, and she was afraid to look up at him. She could see that his fists were clenched at his sides. He might have had a reputation as a wild and rebellious youth, but for all his so-called sins, he'd never been accused of being hot-tempered. She hoped she wasn't setting a new trend in motion.

"But it's true, isn't it?" she insisted stubbornly. She knew she was flirting with danger, but she couldn't seem to stop herself because a part of her longed for just such a confrontation.

"To be quite honest with you, I don't know." He crouched down next to her, his eyes on a level with hers because of the slope of the hillside. "I do know that one of the objects of the game of life is to be at peace with yourself. That means not hurting others and not letting them down." He moved closer to Carly; he seemed to look right through her but at the same time seemed intimately aware of her. "Accomplishments mean nothing if you can't live with yourself."

"Are you at peace?"

"I'm working on it. Believe me, I'm working on it."

His knee went to the ground for balance as his mouth came down on hers. Her hands reached out to automatically brace her body. She couldn't think or protest or do anything but respond to the urgent need they communicated to each other.

His mouth was demanding. He desperately wanted something from her and had somehow decided that only the intimate fusing of mouth upon mouth could deliver it. The blood pounded thickly in her veins when his hands left her shoulders, sliding around her body and tugging her gently to the ground where he lay down beside her, throwing his leg over hers to hold her captive. She didn't resist, didn't want to, as his mouth slanted across hers, his tongue probing for entrance. She moaned a little, realizing that if she allowed him that further intimacy, she would be lost for certain but unable to do anything except relent. She wanted it too badly herself to deny him, and she found herself powerless in the face of his hunger.

When his tongue touched hers, the connection was forged right to the very core of her. Direct hit, she thought dazedly. She half expected to hear sirens and bells going off. Even as she reveled in the sensations of having Deke's strong arms around her, his body half covering hers in the secrecy of the thick, dark night that shielded them both in a fantasy world, her mind reeled with wonder. She'd never known a kiss could contain so many varied sensations. It seemed to her that everything about Deke, his heart and soul, his past and future, his triumphs and his defeats, were all wrapped up in the melding of his lips with hers. She squeezed her eyes tight. Talk about being prone to romantic fantasies.

Deke's mouth left hers, sliding along her cheek and pressing kisses across her temple. She could feel his chest rising and falling with his breathing. She knew hers was also working to replace the breath that he had taken away. Somehow, she couldn't see the kiss as a prelude to rough-and-ready sex the way he had described it to her. He had demanded, yes, but his need had also been a gift to her. She was sure it wasn't often that a man like Deke allowed another person to see anything suggesting vulnerability. She felt pretty vulnerable herself, but oddly enough it didn't contain any elements of being used or taken advantage of. Instead, she felt privileged and proud and strangely humble that she had been able to meet him on this common ground.

"Carly?" His mouth was close to her ear and his voice vibrated there, sending a small shiver along her spine. It snaked down to her stomach then returned up her backbone, only to meet his fingers caressing the nape of her neck.

"Mmm?" She wanted to tell him not to talk, that it would break the spell and kill the beautiful mood that was growing more fragile with every passing second, but she didn't feel she had the right. She also admitted to herself that she was afraid of what he might say or do. She wished she could stop time for a while, just until she could come to terms with everything that was happening so quickly.

"We could zip our sleeping bags together."

She pulled back so she could look into his face. "I know," she said as the situation forced its way back into her consciousness. The dose of reality was painful, but not painful enough to stop her from wondering what she could have been thinking, returning Deke's kiss with such abandon while sitting on the hard ground with the sounds of frogs and bugs all around her. Had she lost her mind completely?

Maybe not, she thought with a wistful smile, still feeling the aftershocks racing through her body. Maybe it was because she was unsure of her allure as a woman in a situation like this, but she knew she wouldn't feel equal to Deke's experience, not to mention his expectations.

She respected herself too much to put herself into that kind of situation, even as her senses were screaming at her that she could handle it, that this time it would be different. What if she found out it was all a horrible mistake like the one she'd almost made with Jean-Claude, who had stirred her senses with promises he hadn't been free to carry out. She knew Deke wasn't engaged, but if something else went wrong she probably wouldn't be able to walk away from it in the morning, and that scared her more than all the rest combined.

"Is that it?" he asked. He pulled back from her, his eyes revealing that he had seen her reservations.

"I just don't think I could be comfortable making love in your sleeping bag." She frowned as she looked down at the object in question. "There's barely enough room in there for me, let alone another person."

His gaze suddenly became hooded and watchful. "That's just logistics," he said, his voice expressionless. "It's something that can be easily remedied . . . if you want it enough."

She shook her head, and the clean night air cleared her mind another notch. "It's silly to start something that has a preordained ending. That might work out perfectly with your plans, but in my book it's just asking for trouble."

"What's wrong with a little trouble?" he asked with a grin. "Especially that kind."

"For you, nothing, I suppose. It fits in with the rest of your life-style, climbing mountains, living on the edge."

He used the ground next to her to push himself to his feet. He thrust his hand through his already-rumpled hair with a weary gesture and his expression reflected an emotion that seemed very close to sorrow or perhaps even defeat. "I don't climb mountains, Carly. I've gotten up into some pretty high altitudes in the Andes, all right, and some of the work I do is dangerous, but not in that way, not with some pure purpose behind it like conquering a virgin mountain peak. I do it solely for the money, what little of it there is."

"Then why did you lead us all to believe that you did?"

"I didn't lead everybody, at least not on purpose. I only implied it in a letter I wrote to Mom one night, and that was after I'd drunk half a bottle of tequila and lost my last *sol* in a game of *churiso*. I guess she told a lot of people."

"Oh."

"Your instincts about me were right in this case, *guapa*." He began walking away. "Good night."

Carly felt her throat catch with emotion. She stared after his retreating figure for a moment before she spoke. "Good night, Deke," she replied, because there was nothing else to say.

Chapter Six

The next morning passed very much like their first one on the trail. Deke seemed to be able to put what had transpired between them the night before out of his mind. He acted as naturally as he always had. He even ruffled her hair in passing, an action that made her gasp, much to her chagrin. Carly tried to adopt the same attitude, but she certainly hadn't been able to achieve the same level of comfort. Obviously he wanted to handle his confession in the time-honored male fashion, by continuing on as though he had never spoken in the first place.

Women were just too sensitive about these emotional kinds of things, she decided as she followed Deke to the cave entrance. Well, she would just have to take a page from Deke's book and quit dwelling on it; otherwise, she would find herself brooding when she should be enjoying the excitement of this quest they were embarked on.

That left her to reflect on what Deke had said to her last night, the words she had replied and the way his body had felt against hers in the soft, secret darkness. Even now she felt small waves of desire wash through her at the thought of making love with him. This was definitely a bad thing for her peace of mind. She wasn't the type to enter into such physical closeness just for a lark.

That was the trouble with romantic types like herself; they tended to fall in love very quickly, or at least they managed to convince themselves that it was love. She had done that once herself, and she didn't want to find herself caught in the same predicament now. Any kind of connection with Deke would have to be purely physical, not to mention finished by the end of the summer when they would both be on their way.

Once again Deke helped her up the side of the hill and into the mouth of the cave. The sun was shining brightly, and it seemed a shame to go from that cheerful summer light to the inky blackness and constant cool temperature under the ground. But the lure of finding the treasure beckoned them on.

"Now I know where they got that phrase blind as a bat," she commented wryly, as the darkness enveloped them. "Speaking of which, how come this cave doesn't have any bats? Not that I'm complaining."

Deke chuckled. "There are no bats because there's no way for them to fly in here." He knelt on the cavern floor. "But see this stuff here. That's guano, bat droppings. It's practically fossilized, that's how long it's been since the entrance of this cave opened directly onto the outside world. I have a hunch that sometime in the past, someone dynamited this entrance closed, to hide it from curious eyes."

"You think Jesse James did it?"

"I don't know. This cave is so huge there's probably another entrance somewhere. Or it might connect up with other caves. That's why we need something more concrete if we hope to find Jesse's loot.'' He smiled at her. ''Still, we're here now, so we might as well give it another shot. Who knows, maybe we'll get lucky.''

He started down the second-largest tunnel opening off the main cavern, unrolling his cord as he went. Carly quickly followed behind, shining her light along the walls of the passage. The sounds of their footsteps were muted in this underground world, and whenever they spoke, their voices seemed to become absorbed into the mass of rock on either side of them.

She remembered a painting of Persephone she had seen in the Louvre. Most artists liked to render the goddess as she was being abducted by Pluto from the sunny field where she'd been picking flowers with her friends, but this particular canvas showed her at home with the god of the underworld in a vast subterranean chamber filled with stalactites and stalagmites. Apart from the eerie strangeness of the rock-encrusted palace, Carly especially remembered the bewildered expression on Persephone's face as she gazed in transfixed wonder at the sights around her. She knew exactly how the poor woman had felt.

The morning passed quickly. In spite of winding their way through endless corridors, they still didn't see a sign of the stashed bank money, even though they did find a veritable wonderland of underground formations. Carly had to admit that there was incredible beauty everywhere. The water-chiseled walls, uneven and craggy, were streaked with mineral stains and onyx deposits. Several of the passages opened into rooms graced with delightful ribbonlike formations.

Various ledges and overhangs had them ducking and laughing as they made their way deeper into the bowels of the earth.

"I'm glad you have that cord to lead us back," Carly commented with a small shiver. "This place feels enough like a tomb as it is without actually becoming one." Her light caught a sinister white gleam in the corner. "Good grief, what's that?"

Deke shone his flashlight in conjunction with hers, and she gasped when the dual beams showed a rather large skeleton. "It looks like bear," he said.

"Ugh." Her voice quivered. "If your dynamite theory is correct, maybe he got caught down here when the cave entrance blew up."

Deke's smile was warm, sending another shiver along her spine, although this one had tinges of warmth to go along with it. "Maybe." He glanced down at his watch. "As much as I'm enjoying the scenery, I think we'd better head out of here. It will take us at least an hour to get back to the cave entrance, and I want to spend the rest of the afternoon looking through the diary."

"Okay."

She looked around for a quiet moment as Deke pounded another eyelet into the wall, fastening their lifeline to it. He had left the cord from the day before as well so they would be aware if they crossed paths, but she hadn't seen any evidence of their previous day's trek. The thought of all those endless corridors, leading to who knew where, was frightening; thank goodness they had their own marked trail to guide them safely out.

Carly was still surprised at how rapidly she was adjusting to life underground now that she had put her mind to it. It really wasn't so bad once you resigned yourself to the pitch blackness that always lurked beyond the edges of your light. She found that if she kept her attention on where she was walking, knowing that Deke was right in front of her with another source of illumination, she was able to sustain an almost lighthearted frame of mind. And his whistling, instead of being jarring or annoying, actually formed a comforting background to her thoughts as they walked along.

When he suddenly stopped, Carly looked up, but not in time to avoid bumping into his back.

"What's the matter?" she asked with a cheerful smile.

He turned to face her. Her smile faded and she gasped when she realized what he'd been looking at. Instead of the cord continuing along the corridor, like a handrail showing them the way back, the twine ended abruptly at the eyelet where the end was tied in a neat bow. She stared at it in disbelief.

"Someone sure has a warped sense of humor," Deke commented darkly.

"You mean someone did this on purpose?" The fact that their marked path was gone hadn't sunk into her brain.

"That cord's been cut and tied like the bow on some damned Christmas present."

Carly could feel the panic bludgeoning its way into her conscious thoughts, even though she would have liked to keep it at bay awhile longer. "No one but Elvie knows we're here," she cried. Even she could hear the note of incipient hysteria in her voice. "Who would want to do such a thing? How are we going to get out?"

"Calm down, honey."

"I can't," she wailed. She didn't even notice the endearment.

He grabbed her by the arms and gave her a shake. "Sure you can. I can't get us out of here if you're carrying on like this. I need you to be quiet and help me."

"I am not carrying on," she said, drawing in a deep, calming breath. "At least not anymore. What are we going to do?"

"Get the hell out of here even though someone seems to have other plans for us. I have to assume that whoever cut that cord also pulled the eyelets out of the wall, since I don't see them. Let's hope we can find the next hole back so we know we're on the right path."

Carly glanced around the cave walls. "That sounds like an impossible task. You don't even know how far it is to the next hole. That's if you can find it among all the natural indentations and crevices."

He dropped his field pack to the ground. "Have you got any better ideas?"

"No."

"All right, then. You'd better turn off your light. We need to conserve the batteries."

She solemnly did as he asked, flicking the switch with a heavy heart. Oddly enough, after her initial frightened reaction, she found that she felt almost calm. She realized that there was an underlying reservoir of fear that she could tap into anytime she wanted, but she was able to ignore its presence by concentrating on what Deke was doing. She had come to trust him absolutely, and she knew he would do everything humanly possible to get them out of here unscathed.

They began the tedious search without further comment. It felt immediately better to be actively doing something geared toward solving their predicament. She tried to occupy her thoughts by filling her mind with passages from Beethoven's Eroica Symphony. She figured maybe the sense of victory inherent in the music would boost her spirits. At least it kept her from brooding.

It seemed like several hours had passed, but it was hard to tell when you were what seemed like fifty fathoms under. They had arrived at an intersection, and they needed to know which path to take.

"I have some candy bars in my field bag if you're hungry." Deke offered, breaking the silence.

"Why is it that people always pull out a candy bar in these kinds of situations?"

Deke continued searching, using both his eyes and his fingertips. She could see the small smile tilting up the corner of his mouth nearest her. "They're portable. Tasty. They give you energy."

She made a face at him. "I don't want one. How can you be so nonchalant?"

"Because getting hysterical isn't going to get us anywhere."

"I know, but it might make me feel better. Possibly even more focused."

"So scream away."

"I can't. You're right, it's too late for screaming now. I should have done it while I was still in the throes of my initial shock. Besides, I might cause an avalanche.''

"I think you mean a cave-in. Hey, I think I found one." He grabbed the flashlight and directed the light at the location. "Yeah, it's from an eyelet screw, all right. We need to continue down this passageway."

"One down, who knows how many to go," she grumbled.

"You've got to be patient, Carly. We're inside way too deep to start running around this maze of a place without knowing the right direction to take. After we find a few more of these holes, our odds of getting the right path will increase. That's when we'll start taking more chances."

"I still don't see why we can't try something a little more productive right now. How about if you tie that cord around my waist and I take a look farther up ahead?"

"And what are you going to find out by doing that?" he demanded. "Until we can get to that last major artery, the one that leads to the entrance, we have no idea what we're looking for. It'll just be a waste of time. I didn't pay attention to every twist and turn we took, did you?"

"No. But inching along at this tortoise pace is driving me crazy."

"I know. I don't like it any better than you do, but I'm trying to keep a cool head and handle our situation in a rational way. If we ever accidentally stray from the trail we followed to get to this point, we'll never get out of here alive."

"You're right. I'm sorry."

"No reason to be." He came close and put his arms around her. "As long as we hang together, we're going to be all right. We've got some candy bars, a couple of apples and a canteen of water. That will last us a long time if we're careful, long enough to get us free."

She slipped her arms around his waist. He was a comforting person to be around in a crisis; she realized she trusted him totally to get them out of here. And yet, as he held her, she felt stirrings of excitement running along her nerve endings. She hadn't known a person could feel fear and desire at the same time. She wanted nothing more than to sink to the ground with Deke and forget about their predicament for a spell. Her practical side warned her against doing that, briskly informing her that the problem would still be there when she drifted back from the physical satiation she knew Deke could provide her. Sometimes she hated what her mother used to label her "good old common sense."

She could feel that Deke's comforting pats on her back were becoming more fluid and caressing. His breathing had slowed and deepened, keeping pace with hers. She closed her eyes for a blissful moment when he squeezed her tightly against his chest, flattening her breasts and sending licks of excitement through the innermost reaches of her body.

"It's too bad we have other priorities right now," he murmured into her hair. "There's nothing I'd like better than a leisurely time-out with you."

So much for her yielding frame of mind. Deke certainly had a romantic way with words. Time-out, indeed. He might think lovemaking was a sport, like football or baseball, but she didn't. She ignored the soft disappointment she could see in his eyes as she pushed away from him. "You're right," she told him with a rueful smile. "We'd better keep on searching. The sooner we find more eyelet holes, the faster we'll get to the entrance."

He looked as though he wanted to say more, but he merely shrugged and turned back to the rough cave wall. Carly did the same. It was slow, frustrating work. Deke figured he had staked the cord out every twenty feet or so, which helped to pinpoint the general area where the next eyelet should be, but not enough to make it an easy task by any means. Still, they continued to make headway, and it was comforting to know that they weren't exactly lost, just moving slow.

"What time is it?" she asked after another interminable length of time had passed.

"Seven-thirty."

"You mean it's already dark outside?"

"Yeah."

"Oh." Her fingers automatically kept on searching for the next tiny opening. "So we've been in here over six hours."

"That's right."

"Who would want to do this to us, Deke?"

"That's the question I've been asking myself all afternoon."

"And what did you answer yourself?"

"I don't have an answer." He threw out his arms in frustration. "No one knows we're out here. No one should even give a damn that we are. It's not hunting season, and there's no place to fish for miles."

"What if someone saw the car?" she asked, her eyes wide with apprehension.

He shook his head. "No. Even if someone spotted the car, that's a couple of hours of hiking time away, which means he'd need to be good enough at reading trails to know which direction we went."

"Suppose he followed us. Suppose he's been spying on us all along."

"I would have heard him, Carly. It's just too far-fetched to think that someone was spying on us when no one knew about the map or the bank stash."

"If he wasn't spying on us, how did he find the opening to the cave? It's impossible to see unless you know where to look."

He sighed. "I just don't know. But I damn well aim to find out what the hell is going on once we're out of here."

Carly shivered as a glint of satisfaction chased up her spine. She wouldn't want to be the person who had tried to mess with Deke. She didn't think he would be the type to shrug something like this off. As for herself, she figured she would be so grateful to leave this rocky underground world behind, she might be tempted to let bygones be bygones.

She couldn't remember a time when her legs and back hadn't been aching. She stifled a small groan as she raised her arms to resume her meticulous searching. The pads of her fingers felt so raw she wondered if she would be able to feel one of the elusive eyelet holes even if she came across it, and her eyes were tired from holding them wide open as she tried to see around the wavering shadows caused by the various parts of her body. She wasn't sure she'd ever be able to close them without using her fingers to pull down her strained eyelids.

In spite of her dogged input, Deke had managed to discover almost all of the eyelet holes. Still, she didn't really want to rest. The sooner they found more holes to point them in the right direction, the sooner they would be out of this black pit and she could resume normal blinking once again.

Suddenly Deke gave a great shout, jarring her so quickly out of her woeful contemplations that she hugged the rough wall for balance.

"What? What is it?"

"I don't believe this." He met her startled eyes and pointed to a spot on the wall just at the edge of their circle of light.

"Oh my goodness," she said, hardly daring to believe what she was seeing. There nestled primly on the cave wall was an eyelet with the end of a rope tied to it. From there it continued as though it had never been cut.

"It's not a trick, is it?" she asked warily. She found she didn't trust anything anymore. Except for Deke, of course.

"How could it be? We've been followiong the holes all along and this is just picking up where we left off."

"Now I'm really confused. It almost seems as though whoever cut the cord only wanted to delay us, not get us lost completely." She frowned indignantly. "Whoever it was, he was lucky we didn't lose our heads and start dashing madly around looking for a way out."

"He sure was." Deke's mouth thinned for a moment. "Come on, let's go."

He picked up the field pack and the flashlight, then grabbed her by the arm, hustling her along the corridor toward the entrance. She knew it must be her imagination but she could almost smell the fresh air seeping in from the outside.

When they finally reached the lofty cavern that meant the exit was just ahead, Carly squealed in delight. Deke dropped her arm for a moment and she didn't miss her chance, bolting for the opening like a rabbit being chased by the hounds of hell. Just before she got there, Deke tackled her to the ground, knocking the air from her lungs.

"Ooph." She squirmed wildly beneath him. "What do you think you're doing, Deacon Baxter?"

"What do you think you're doing?" he retorted in a low voice. "Are you crazy? Whoever cut the rope might be out there, just waiting for us."

Carly felt the tears filling her eyes. She was at the end of her own rope, especially if she didn't get out of here immediately. Nothing seemed as important as that, not even the fact that someone might be waiting for them outside.

She continued to struggle. "Let me go."

"Carly," he said urgently. "Carly, calm down. Come on, sweetheart, it can't be as bad as all that to stay in here another five minutes or so while I scout out the opening."

She didn't answer him, although she blew out her breath rebelliously.

"Come on, you've survived everything else so far, haven't you?" He quirked his eyebrows at her. "You even survived me coming on to you without any permanent damage, didn't you?"

If he hoped to inject humor into this situation, it wasn't going to work. She was dirty and tired and in no mood for light repartee about anything, especially that particular subject.

"That's why there wasn't any damage, because you were 'coming on' to me," she muttered in a tight whisper. She was grateful to Deke, more than she could say, for getting them this far, but she couldn't seem to stop herself from continuing to goad him, even from her vulnerable position beneath his heavier, stronger male body. "If you had asked me to make love it might have been a different story."

They glared at each other for several long moments, neither of them willing to yield the point. The tension that was never far from the surface escalated until even the air around them seemed to be charged. There were a lot of emotions trying to crowd their way into that single chamber and nowhere for them to dissipate.

Deke was the first one to break the impasse. "Get real, sweetheart, and quit trying to feed me that line about semantics making the difference, because I'm not buying it. You can call it whatever you want, but it's still the same thing, sexual behavior between consenting adults."

"I'm so glad we're having this little discussion," she said, her smile tight as she clamped down on the small inner voice that told her she should hold her tongue, that this exchange was unnecessary, that they should be working together. She struggled against his hands pinning her down, but he was unyielding. She hated to admit it to herself, but his words were hurting her and she found herself striking back with all the weapons she could conjure up on such short notice. "It's certainly cured me forever of any desire I might have had to take you up on your oh-so-romantic offer."

He snorted in disdain. "You just want to candy-coat something that's as natural and elemental as the wind and the sky. Women are always doing that. It doesn't change anything just because you call it by a different name."

He shoved her hands away, freeing them as he rolled off her, and immediately sat up on his haunches. He was still looming above her, but she managed to scramble to her feet, backing away from him until she felt the cold stone wall against her spine.

"I could have given you the romantic words you wanted to hear," he continued in a rough voice. "I could have had you begging me to make love to you. But I felt it was a dishonest thing to do, using your own weakness against you like that."

"It's not a weakness, it's a preference," she retorted through clenched teeth. "Like chocolate or vanilla."

She continued to clamp her teeth together since she was afraid she might start crying in anger and frustration if she didn't. Of course, she assured herself that she was too civilized for such infantile behavior, but such rational advice was having little effect on her raging impulses. In fact, it seemed to inflame them even more.

She didn't have anything to throw so she finally allowed herself the satisfaction of sliding down the cave wall until she was sitting on the floor, her arms crossed defiantly over her chest as she stared at a point away from Deke's face. "Go ahead, play Indian scout. I'll wait right here."

When he didn't answer right away, she looked up to find that he was shaking his head in a puzzled fashion. "I still can't believe you really mean it when you tell me that's all it would take, a little sweet talk."

"No, that's not what I mean to tell you at all." She blew out her breath in exasperation. "Some men naturally understand a woman's psychic makeup and some don't."

"I see. And I suppose Frenchmen belong to the former category and I belong to the latter."

Her shrug left him to draw his own conclusions. Deke watched her solemnly for a moment before he walked to the cave entrance. He drew in a calming breath, deciding he needed at least a few moments to get his libido under control. Women, he muttered to himself under his breath with a disgruntled frown before dropping to the ground. He didn't know how they got their heads stuffed with the ungodly amount of romantic nonsense that always seemed to fill them.

He paused for a moment, trying to ignore the unfriendly vibrations that were emanating from Carly as she sat stiffly against the wall staring straight ahead. Maybe she really did want him, maybe she couldn't allow herself to express desire for him until he convinced her that it was safe to do so with the soft words of love she wanted to hear. He couldn't have been mistaken about her response to him.

He crawled carefully on his hands and knees until he was even with the cave opening. Lord, that outside air felt like heaven, he thought as he allowed the cool Ozark mountain air to fill his lungs. He needed to drag his mind to the task ahead, but his attention was still consumed with Carly. Safe, he thought to himself derisively. Who in the wild blue yonder was ever safe when it came to relationships. It was a simple fact of life that you had to lay your head on the block when it came time to risk your body and emotions with someone, whether you were jumping into the sack or "making love."

He grimaced. It didn't look good for the home team, he reflected wryly, glancing back at her. She hadn't moved. He wasn't sure if he could compromise his principles by using the tactics she so desperately wanted, mostly because he felt that feeding the woman a line, promising her love and eternal devotion if you didn't mean it, was cheating, and he'd always considered himself too honest and aboveboard to resort to that. With him, a woman knew exactly what she was getting. So why did he feel this compulsion to force the issue with Carly, to compromise his principles in order to have her in his bed?

He chastised himself, realizing that the answer was simple and obvious. He wanted her more than he'd ever wanted any woman in his entire life. He ate, slept and breathed his need to have her. The stakes had become higher than he was used to, and he suddenly found himself ready to sell his principles down the river in order to possess her. He'd always thought that women held all the cards when it came to relationships and sex; men asked and women accepted or rejected. He'd never fully realized that males also wielded some powerful weapons.

He felt her glance over at him, and he couldn't help but shake his head at his thoughts, a reluctant half smile softening his features. "What are you waiting for?" she demanded.

He shrugged. "Nothing. I'm just feeling light-headed at the moment."

"Too much fresh air?" she asked sweetly.

"Too much enlightenment."

He could tell that she wanted to question him further, but she obviously didn't want to give him the satisfaction of knowing she was curious. It didn't take a genius to realize that she was still annoyed with him over his comments. She had made it clear that she didn't care for his entire attitude, but he hoped that was something that could be remedied with honesty between them. He certainly intended to try. Suddenly it had become very important that he attempt to bridge the barriers between their very different outlooks.

"Don't move from that spot," he called softly over his shoulder. "I should be back in five minutes." He lowered himself to his belly, keeping his head low as he began to crawl out.

Carly shivered as she watched his feet disappear through the opening. She could feel the freshness of the outside air, and it had a cool bite to it that hadn't been there last night. She hugged herself more tightly, trying to stay warm now that the worst seemed to be over. She found that her body felt lethargic and her spirits let down.

Not wanting to occupy her mind with dismal imaginings of what might or might not be happening outside, she thought about her relationship with Deke. Why should she care that he was only "coming on" to her, that he only wanted a tumble in the hay? Hadn't she already suspected it? That was the trouble with men like that; once you told them no they got all surly and lost interest in you as a person. What did she want with a guy who was only interested in sex, anyway? She had only herself to blame. She was the fool who had concluded that they were getting along well, and now she was the idiot who had hurt feelings because she realized it was all an illusion in her mind.

Deke's kiss wasn't an illusion, however, and the memory of it floated tauntingly through her brain as she moved restlessly on the hard ground. Back in high school it had been the excitement of forbidden fruit that had stirred her more than anything else. Now she actually felt a physical ache that yearned to be filled by having him touch her and kiss her. Just the thought of such acts brought an embarrassed flush to her face. She'd never thought of herself as the kind of female who would react so strongly to sexual provocation.

But it was more than that. Deke exuded sex and sin with his looks, his cavalier attitude, his muscled physique. She even liked him when he was sweaty and breathing hard; she had no idea when the vision of a glistening torso had begun to turn her on, but it had happened sometime between last Tuesday and today. Drat Deacon Baxter, anyway. It must be true that rogues were irresistible to women, because she was finding herself helpless before his sensual spell.

How could she have suddenly become so carnal when she had always envisioned herself wrapped in the arms of a man who smelled of expensive cologne, whose hair was styled and whose clothes spelled success. In other words, a civilized man. She punched the air in frustration, shaking her head in disgust. She'd known Deke was going to be trouble, but she had never imagined this kind of trouble. If she wasn't careful, she might find herself detouring from the strategic career path she had chosen for herself and straight into sexual thralldom.

She had barely finished yelling at herself when Deke materialized before her eyes.

"It seems safe enough for the moment. I didn't see signs of anyone."

Carly pushed herself to her feet. "Good. Then let's go."

"Wait a minute. I said I didn't see signs of anyone, but that doesn't mean there's no one out there."

She stared at him apprehensively.

"Which means that we're going to spend the night right here."

She wanted to protest, but she knew he was right. No one could sneak up on them in here, and they would be safe until morning. "Okay," she agreed.

"Good." He was staring at her as though she'd turned into food and he was a starving man. Awareness of the boundaries of her body and his and their relative positions in relation to each other in this small space shot through her in a powerful surge.

"So, what now?"

"I'll slip outside again and get our sleeping bags and the rest of our stuff."

"Great. I never thought I'd be grateful for a sleeping bag, but I don't think I'd like sleeping on this hard floor. Can we have a fire in here? No, I suppose not, anyone would be able to see the light from it for miles. I hope you have something to eat that doesn't need to be cooked."

She knew she was babbling, but she couldn't seem to stop. And all the while Deke was looking at her in that new, intense way that turned her bones to marmalade.

"What's the matter?" she finally asked with her last rush of breath. "I agreed without a fuss, what else do you want?"

His smile in response to that was positively unholy, especially assisted as it was by the wavering shadows inside the cave. She felt a wild compulsion to either scream or throw herself into his arms. Either course was suicide, but whatever the sentiment behind it, that look was surely intense.

"You'd better not ask leading questions like that, Carly," he said softly.

He dropped to his hands and knees and disappeared out the entrance while she continued to stare after him mutely.

She stood there for the longest time, the blood surging in her veins in an anticipation she couldn't quell—nor was she sure she wanted to. Deke returned, dumping the sleeping bags and other paraphernalia onto the ground in front of her like an offering even as he continued to stare at her. Her suicidal impulses were still operational, because she found herself demanding, "Why do you keep looking at me like that?"

"Like what?"

"Come on, Deke. You know what I mean."

He grinned. "Yeah, I do. I look like I want to devour you. That's because I do."

She closed her eyes for a composure-gathering moment and swallowed hard. "When did you come to that conclusion?"

"I've felt that way all along, but I finally decided to let it all hang out, as the expression goes. I'm sure the French have a much nicer way of saying it, but that's still the bottom line. We came mighty close to becoming permanently entombed not too long ago. Something like that makes a guy take a closer look at his options."

"And just what am I supposed to say to that?"

He shrugged congenially, bending down to move his backpack. "Nothing."

"Then what do you want me to do about it?"

She actually saw the pupils of his eyes flare wider in reaction to her statement as he glanced back at her over his shoulder. Blue iris and black pupil combined in a rich midnight color whose depths threatened to swallow her whole. "Well, I'd love for you to reciprocate, but I can see you're not quite ready for that. Therefore, you can do whatever moves you. As for me, I'm trying the totally honest approach by letting the way I feel show."

"I see."

"I'm not sure if you really do. Let me explain." He tossed one of the sleeping bags against the far wall. "Last night after you told me off, I thought long and hard about some of the things we'd talked about, especially how we each felt about the so-called game of love. And I decided that while I was so righteously scorning the French for playing games with their sweet words and gestures, I was playing a game as well. Except that my game was at the complete opposite end of the spectrum.''

He carried his pack to the sleeping bag, set it off to one side, then began unrolling the material with a casual flip of his wrists as he looked up to gauge her reaction. He seemed satisfied with it so he continued. "My game plan has always been to act any damned way I pleased. I was especially happy if my behavior was so raw it made other people uncomfortable. Who needed redeeming social graces, anyway? Certainly not me. That way I could tell myself that the woman wanted what I had to offer because she was willing to put up with all that to get it, and it left my conscience clear.''

"So what makes what you're doing now any different?"

"Simple. Now I'm just acting the way I feel and saying the things I want without straying into either extreme camp.'' His smile was crooked.

She remained silent, unable to summon up a smile or a frown or any of the other human expressions usually required in response to another's conversation. The trouble was she hadn't a thing to say because he had shocked the fire right out of her. It sounded oh-so-rational, this new open attitude of his, but she recognized it for what it was—the most dangerous masculine ploy of all.

"You could do the same thing, you know," he added.

This time she managed a grimace. "Thanks. I'll keep it in mind.''

"You're welcome." He threw himself down onto the waterproof nylon surface. "So, how about some dinner? I'm starving, aren't you?"

"Famished," she replied almost absentmindedly.

He handed her a can of stew and the opener. "We're going to have to eat it cold tonight," he said cheerfully.

"Are you going to watch every move I make?"

He tilted his head, eyeing her consideringly, then nodded. "Absolutely."

"Great." She glared at him as she sat down on her rolled-up sleeping bag, and spread her legs in front of her for balance. His eyes caught the glare from the flashlight, and the desire she saw there took her breath away. He wasn't kidding about any of this.

Carly took a deep breath, suddenly realizing that her lungs had been starving for air during this entire interlude with Deke. The man was a menace, no doubt about it. She wanted to grab on to what he offered with both hands. She couldn't believe that it was just an act; he seemed so sincere, his gaze so straightforward.

He hadn't promised her anything, either, she reflected as she laboriously turned the handle of the opener. Setting the lid aside, she picked up the fork Deke had left for her and began to eat. She couldn't think straight, the usually clear river of her mental processes seemed to be stopped up with mud and debris. He was going to drive her crazy. And yet, a small, logical voice insisted he wasn't doing anything underhanded or illegal. He just wasn't following predictable social customs. Which still made him a rebel in her mind.

She wasn't foolish enough to believe that just because he had changed his methods he was about to settle down. Leopards didn't change their spots and neither did men like Deke. South America would surely lure him back. Or some other place. Even if he did fall in love, he would never be able to settle down to an existence that simply included a family and a home. That kind of life lacked the carefree open-ended life-style that nourished the soul of a man like him. And Carly was not the kind of woman who could be content with a part-time lover.

She put the can of stew aside. It was decidedly unappealing, and besides, she found her appetite was nonexistent. She shivered, rubbing her arms to stimulate the circulation.

"If you'd like, I can keep you warm tonight, Carly," he offered, his expression perfectly serious.

Her smile was brief. "I'm sure I'll be fine."

"I'm not so sure about that. I wasn't expecting it to get this cold in June. Those sleeping bags are only rated for sixty degrees."

She turned to look at him. "You don't think it will get any colder than that, do you?"

He shrugged. "Hard to say. Anyway, as I just said, you don't have to worry about it, I'll keep you warm."

She didn't need to ask him to clarify his meaning; she knew exactly what he wanted because she wanted it, too. Her time of reckoning was drawing too close for comfort, and now that it was almost here she found that she wanted to run away like the lowliest coward. She gratefully accepted the canteen of water he held out to her, trying to keep her gaze semiaverted from his without being too conspicuous about it. Of course, he saw right through her ploy.

"Why won't you look at me?" he asked softly. He stuck his fork into the stew and set the can aside.

She opened her mouth to reply, but he didn't let her. "And don't say you're not avoiding my eyes."

"Okay, I won't."

"Am I making you uncomfortable?"

She shrugged. "A little."

"I think it's more than a little." He got up and came around to her side. She still refused to acknowledge his presence, even though it was a futile gesture. Instead, she stared at his boots on the hard dirt-and-rock floor. He had propped the flashlight along the far wall so that it wouldn't shine directly into their faces. He now appeared like a huge black silhouette, looming over her.

"You know what? I think that you want me, too, otherwise you would have already told me to get lost." He knelt down until his face was only inches away from hers. "You're too honest to do otherwise, isn't that right, Carly?"

As much as she'd been avoiding his gaze earlier, her eyes now refused to leave his, even though the contact made her stomach swoop and dip like a ride on the Tilt-A-Whirl.

"I also think you're the kind of woman who likes a man to sweep her off her feet. Everything you've said about the subject implies just that."

He grasped her arm and pulled her from the top of the bag, then leaned down to begin unzipping it. It sounded like fingernails on a blackboard to her and she swallowed. His voice drowned all other noises out.

"Now, I'm not sure I can do it just the way you like, but I'm going to give it my best shot. And I can't say the words in French, but even in English the sentiment is the same." His lips quirked in an appealing smile. "Besides, most of what I want to tell you doesn't require words."

She watched in total fascination as he spread out her sleeping bag on the ground, unable to move or protest. He unpeeled the layers so that the flannel she usually slept against was open to the night air, its tender inner core exposed. She smiled, thinking Deke had zeroed in on *her* inner being, caressing it, crooning to it and coaxing it from the deep, secret place where it had lain hidden for so long.

He pulled her down alongside him, and she fell into a dreamlike haze of pleasure because he wanted her enough and cared enough about her feelings to study her and discover her secret longings. Even the frosty chill tinging the air couldn't penetrate the place where she was now.

Deke covered her body with his and began kissing her throat, his mouth moving to the sensitive juncture where her neck met her shoulders. He moved the material of her blouse and sweater aside so his lips could test the warm skin at the base of her throat where her pulse fluttered. "It's cold in here, but I'm going to keep you so warm you won't even notice."

Carly just stared back at him. She wanted to say nothing that might break the sensuous spell he was weaving around her. Her arms rested beside her. Deke stroked them just before he lifted them to encircle his own neck. When she obliged, he finally kissed her.

She let out a small sigh as his mouth settled onto hers. How odd that she should feel such a sense of homecoming at the contact. She realized that they must have been building toward this moment longer than she had thought. He tasted like the outdoors—cool, untamed and mysteriously foreign—yet at the same time his mouth was burning hot like the sun on the desert floor. His body pressed hers into the ground, and she found she was glad of that hard surface beneath her since it served to keep her in closer contact with every part of him. His hands caressed her through her clothes, making her twist and turn beneath him with the sheer pleasure of his touch. She wanted more, she wanted him to touch her naked flesh. A distant part of her mind wondered how her inhibitions had flown away so quickly since she was usually quite shy with men when it came to revealing anything beneath the social mask.

He shifted his weight a little to one side, his hands continuing to stroke along the length of her body, shaping her breasts beneath their heavy covering of sweater and blouse, kneading her hips and stomach with strong, sure fingers. "Carly, sweetheart, take your clothes off."

She didn't respond immediately, even though she wanted to feel his naked flesh against her own. She needed him to take control and he didn't disappoint her.

"Here, wait a minute. I don't want you to get cold."

She felt him reach behind them, and then she heard a dragging sound. She understood what he was up to when she saw him pull his sleeping bag alongside. He kept one arm around her even as he somehow managed to unzip it, only leaving her a moment while he sat up so he could spread its heavy, warm weight over them.

When she felt him pull her into a sitting position, she wondered how he could have ever said he was rugged and unpolished. Her mind tried to signal her mouth to smile, but it was too busy returning Deke's hungry little kisses to pay any heed. She wanted to ask him if this was what he considered direct and all-American, because if it was, refined would never have the same lure for her again.

He reached down for the hem of her sweater, pulling it over her head in a smooth, gentle motion. His fingers went immediately to the buttons of her blouse, as though he didn't want to waste a precious second in the process of uncovering her. Their eyes met, and she was shaken to the core to see the naked longing revealed in the depths of his gaze. Had she really inspired a man like Deke to that kind of unreasoning passion? She smiled tentatively at him, but his mouth remained taut even as his gaze softened. He was a man beyond the point of no return, his expression told her.

"Please don't stop me now," he whispered in a ragged voice. He stroked her cheek, his soft gesture taking away some of the fear that suddenly arose in her at the harshness of his expression. His naked, unchecked desire was almost frightening to behold, she thought to herself with a small shiver, especially when she had never in her life experienced anything as elemental.

"I won't, Deke," she said, wanting to promise him everything, longing to give him anything he wanted if only he would keep looking at her in that thrillingly primitive way. "I don't want to."

He slid the blouse from her shoulders, his hands trembling. Carly was awed at the need in him that made him both vulnerable and powerful at the same time. She felt an answering response building up inside her, until she thought she would explode if she didn't touch and caress him the way he was doing to her. She'd always believed that the man was the one with all the sex drive, that his powerful feelings pushed lovemaking to its final consummation, but she suddenly found that it wasn't true, at least not with this man. She'd been passive long enough, allowing Deke to set the pace and deal with all the uncertainty of her response as he laid his soul bare before her. He deserved to know that he too was desired, that he too was inspiring longings and feelings that went far beyond everyday interaction.

She pushed his hands away as they reached around behind her for the fastening of her bra. "No," she said simply. Ignoring the chill of the night air which she could feel but which didn't seem to affect her, she tugged his sweatshirt over his head, baring his beautiful torso to the weakening glow of the flashlight. With his assistance, she unfastened his pants and drew them over his hips, taking his briefs along with them. Now he was totally naked and totally, deliciously hers to command.

He looked up at her and his eyes were smiling. "You have me in your power, *guapa*. Now what are you going to do with me?" he asked, his voice reflecting deep satisfaction at his predicament.

She ran her hands along his chest, her fingers curling in the hair that they found there. She felt like an Amazon warrior whose conquest was laid out like a sacrifice before her. And yet she was conquered, too. "I'm going to make love to you," she told him, and her words made her suddenly a little shy.

"Say it to me in French."

"Je voudrais faire amour avec toi," she murmured, her lips caressing each soft syllable as it left her mouth. It was a shockingly erotic experience so she added more. *"J'ai envie de te caresser."*

"What does that mean?" he asked in a husky voice.

"I want to caress you."

"Yes," he said, pulling her down beside him. He made short work of her jeans and panties, somehow managing to zip the two sleeping bags together while he did it. "Oh, yes."

He scooped her into his arms, pulling her against him and rolling back and forth inside the sleeping bag in an exuberant demonstration of his feelings. His body was hot to the touch, and the delicious smell of his skin filled her senses. She laughed joyously along with him. He paused at the sound, and although she couldn't see his expression because their movements had thrust them deeply inside the sleeping bag, she could sense the change of direction in his intentions. The time for playfulness was over. When his mouth came down on hers for a second time, it wasn't gentle, but she had no desire to be gentle. She wanted to answer his passion with her own.

And she did. She reveled in every aspect of the act of love. Things that had previously diverted her passion now delighted her. The sounds Deke made when she kissed him, the feel of his sweat-slicked body as it moved with such power against hers, the shocking intimacy when he slid into the most inviolable reaches of her body, his rhythmic strokes that lifted her off the ground as she strove to meet them. The sheer physicality of the act only emphasized for her the emotional and spiritual nature of the bond they were forging as they tried to meld their bodies together into one flesh.

She had never experienced anything like it. The cumulative effect made her head spin and her senses spiral out of control. Deke's ragged breathing told her that he was on the edge as well, but he held back just long enough for her to explode in pinpoint bursts of light before he cried out her name and followed her into the realm of physical satiation and emotional bliss.

She drifted slowly back from the place she'd been, her body drowsy and complete, her eyes closed. The heat they had generated still filled the inside of the sleeping bag, trapped against the flannel lining. Carly allowed the sigh to escape her lips, knowing she could withhold nothing from him, not now, not while the blackness of the night and the newness of their coming together still beguiled her.

"Are you all right?" he asked, his breath tickling her ear.

"Yes." She could feel the smile stretching her lips from their slack repose.

"I warned you that I was a rough, unrefined kind of guy."

Her smile widened. "You did."

"I told you I didn't know what to say, how to be romantic." He stroked her arm and shoulder with gentle, erratic, heartfelt motions.

Carly lifted herself onto one elbow so she could look into his face. "If you had been any more romantic, we would have had to worry about nuclear meltdown. You are lethal and should come with an appropriate warning for the unwary woman."

"You're the one who's lethal, Carly. I...it's never been like that for me."

Then what are you going to do about it, she wanted to ask, but decided that tomorrow would be soon enough for facing such thorny questions. Besides, she didn't want to give in to the typical female anxiety usually felt in these vulnerable situations. She wasn't prepared for the answers, anyway, so she placed several kisses along the firm line of his jaw then settled down beside him. He responded immediately by drawing her closer.

"Will we be warm enough here, without our clothes?" she asked.

He chuckled. "Sure. Our combined body heat will be more than ample. I don't think the temperature's going to drop much further before the morning."

"Okay. If you say so."

"I appreciate the vote of confidence." He rubbed his cheek against the crown of her head. "Are you sorry, Carly?"

She drew in a deep breath and then told the truth as she was living it in her heart that very moment, squeezing out thoughts of both the past and the future from her mind. "No." She snuggled down against his warmth and was soon fast asleep.

It took Deke longer to settle into slumber. For one thing, he was enjoying the feel of Carly in his arms too much to lose awareness too quickly. She lay tight against his body, and when he flexed the muscles in his arms, she responded with a little sigh, wiggling her bottom closer into the cradle of his thighs. It made him hard and caused his loins to ache, but it was such a pleasurable ache that he didn't mind at all. He wondered if she would fuss if he woke her up again and made love to her. In a little while he would see how she responded to another overture, but for now he was content to stay just this side of heaven.

The unsettling part was that there was an undercurrent to his feelings for Carly, something besides physical satiation, that had never been there before. He had always managed to walk away from sticky emotional situations because he was always on the move, and the women he had met up with knew he wouldn't be hanging around for any finales. Now it seemed as though fate was having a good laugh at his expense because this time it was the woman who intended to move on. Oh, yes, this time she was the one who had places to go and worlds to conquer.

His mouth tightened for a moment, then it relaxed into a smile. Maybe she was leaving too soon for his liking, he reflected, but for the time being she belonged to him, whether she agreed with that assessment or not. He smiled grimly as he reached out to turn off the flashlight. He fully intended to meet the challenge of their attraction in spite of its ultimate futility.

Chapter Seven

Carly awoke instantly from a dead sleep. She'd been dreaming of ethereal, kaleidoscopic visions whose exact meaning she couldn't grasp, but she knew immediately where she was and why she felt so contented. She opened her eyes to find that she had no idea what time it was, although she knew it had to be past dawn since she was able to see light creeping into the cave. In any case, it felt much too early to think about getting up. She closed her eyes and enjoyed the murky darkness as it caressed her eyelids.

The temperature had dropped a good fifteen degrees below the normal weather expected at this time of year, but Carly didn't let it bother her. From her vantage point inside the warm cocoon of the sleeping bag, she was immune to the capricious summer cold front that had swooped down on them from the north. Deke's arm lay across her back, and his left leg pressed heavily into the backs of her thighs, pinning her against the ground and effectively assuring both of them that she wasn't moving anywhere without his knowledge.

She wriggled a little just to see if he was awake, but he didn't move a muscle. The sound of his deep, even breathing convinced her that he was sound asleep and that she could enjoy the exquisite physical pleasure of just lying next to him, reliving the events of the past night without interruption.

He had made love to her a second time, long after she had fallen asleep beside him. She had never been awakened with kisses and caresses like that, had never really spent the night with a man before. It was like nothing she had ever experienced, coming into full consciousness in such a slow, erotic fashion and feeling her naked limbs sliding against Deke's flesh. She'd known there would be pleasure in such a procedure, but she had never realized the full, melting extent of it.

Deke had been oddly gentle and careful with her that second time, or at least he had until she had moaned and moved her hips in counterpoint rhythm to his. Then he had seemed to lose all control. She had liked that part even more, using everything she could think of to further his pleasure and drive him over the edge. A knowing smile curved her lips as she remembered the sounds he had made, while flashes of some of the sensations she had experienced replayed through her nerve endings.

"I think we're going to find Jesse's stash soon," Deke whispered in her ear. "I'm starting to feel pretty lucky."

Carly felt herself blushing now that she knew he was awake. She couldn't believe after all they had shared together throughout the night that it was possible for her to feel embarrassed, but she found that in what passed for the light of day she wasn't immune to that emotion. She had never experienced a true morning-after, so she supposed it wasn't all that unusual to feel uncomfortable about being naked with a man, especially when she realized that she had no robe to slip on and no welcoming bathroom to modestly disappear into while she got dressed.

"What do we do next?" she asked, trying to sound nonchalant.

"You mean as an encore after yesterday's little fiasco?" He reached down to squeeze her bottom affectionately. Carly squealed and he chuckled. "I don't know, I haven't thought that far ahead. I brought some wood from outside last night so we could make a small fire this morning." He gave her another quick squeeze. "I think we're going to need it."

"Be my guest," she said.

He slid out of the sleeping bag and into the bone-chilling cold of the cavern. Even in this dim light, Carly could see that his skin immediately erupted into goose bumps, but the long, smooth, sexy lines of his body still set her heart pounding. He quickly reached for his jeans and pulled a sweatshirt over his head, then bent down to begin building the fire, just to the left of the opening so that some of the smoke would be pulled along the high cavern ceiling and some would drift outside. A small plume of white rose and soon a nice crackling blaze was burning, filling the cavern with a beautiful orange-red glow. Carly could feel its heat on her face.

He squatted down on his haunches in front of the pile of clothes she had so eagerly shed last night. "Now, let's see, what do you need," he began teasingly. He held up her jeans. "These for a start," he said, tucking them under his arm. "And these," he indicated her blouse and sweater, adding them to his cache.

"Mmm, what have we here?" He held up her bikini panties. "These are better than nice."

Carly groaned as he picked up the flashlight and turned it on for a better look. After spending over two years in France, she had become somewhat of an underwear connoisseur. How could she help it when shopping in the lingerie capital of the world? Now that Deke was inspecting the result of one particularly intense shopping spree at the Galeries Lafayette, fingering the lace-trimmed bikini panties, holding them this way and that as he carefully examined every aspect of the delicate workmanship, she realized how utterly inappropriate they were for life on the trail. If she'd owned a more practical pair, she would have worn them. Besides, she had never planned on being in any situation more rugged than riding the Paris Metro.

"They look good enough to eat," he said, brushing the silky material against his face, his gaze electrically connected to hers. "It was too dark last night to see what I was taking off you."

"Give them...to me," she said. She had to clear her throat after the second word. He relinquished them without a fuss, and she quickly clutched them to her chest beneath the covers.

"And this," Deke said, holding up her bra, managing to use both hands to do it, even though he still held the flashlight propped beneath one arm. "I certainly would have taken my time removing this little item." He grinned mischievously. "I'm short-circuiting my brain trying to imagine what this looks like against your skin."

He held the lacy little confection up to the beam of light, running his fingers over the material, studying the construction with a fascinated expression on his face. The roughness of his long, tanned fingers silhouetted against the creamy color and expensive texture caused her insides to tighten in response. Even two years in Paris hadn't prepared her for Deke's heads-up attitude and hands-on approach to the morning-after.

"I suppose it's too cold to ask you to model them for me this morning," he commented regretfully.

"Yes, definitely," she agreed as if that were the only thing holding her back. She held out her hand for the rest of her clothes and he gave them to her with some reluctance. "What's for breakfast?"

"Two-day-old doughnuts and coffee." His expression was thoughtful as he continued to stare at her. "Is that stuff from Paris?"

She managed to squirm into her panties. "Yes," she said breathlessly. It was hard work getting dressed in a sleeping bag, even a double one, but she was quickly finding out that necessity was the mother of invention. Before she could say Moulin Rouge she had the bra on as well. Cold air rushed inside every time she moved, and she was beginning to shiver. Deke hadn't even bothered to put on his shoes and socks, but he looked warm and vital as he strode around the cavern, picking up stray objects. When he bent down to retrieve the coffeepot, she grabbed her chance and slipped into her blouse.

"Coffee sure sounds good," she said cheerfully, deciding it was now or never. She quickly slid out of the sleeping bag and stood up, managing to grab her jeans and get one foot into them before Deke turned around. His eyes lit up at the sight of her and he crossed the small distance between them with a pouncing motion that set her heart pounding.

"Mmm," he said as he pulled her against him. His hands were all over her back and hips in quick preliminary strokes before they honed in on their target. He rubbed and caressed her silk-covered bottom as though he couldn't get enough of the feel of her.

"I didn't know lingerie could turn me on like this," he said with a muffled groan. His hands followed the contours of the material where it was cut high along her thighs before returning again to her behind, stroking and squeezing until she felt hot enough to disregard the temperature. Her skin was flushed, and she could feel the heat coming right through Deke's sweatshirt along with the warm, tangy scent of his skin.

A sudden loud hissing from the fire brought them to an abrupt halt. "Damn," Deke muttered as he let her go. "It's the coffee." He grabbed one of his socks, and using it as a potholder quickly pulled the coffeepot over to the side of the camp grate that wasn't directly over the fire. Even so he managed to burn himself. "Damn it," he said again as his eyes met hers. He was breathing hard.

She slipped into her jeans while she had the opportunity. Even though he'd only been gone from her a brief minute, the cold was already penetrating through her heated flesh.

"I guess we'd better get going, huh?"

"I knew it! I knew bringing a woman along would be a disaster." He grunted as he sat down and began thrusting his feet into his socks. "How am I supposed to concentrate on anything but trying to get my hands on you now that I know what's underneath those jeans?" he asked her. She hoped it was a rhetorical question. "I'll probably end up maiming myself for life."

"Well, excuse me," she retorted in mild amusement at being blamed for his inattention to the details of camp life. "No one asked you to inspect my lingerie."

"It was my pleasure." He jammed his left foot into his hiking boot. "Leave it to you to wear French silk lingerie instead of plain cotton underwear."

"It's the only kind I own." She tried to keep a straight face as she shrugged. "I wish I could say I wore it just to drive you crazy, but I happen to like the way it feels against my skin."

He groaned long and loud, shaking his head. "Women were born to drive men crazy."

She pulled her sweater on over her head wondering if she even needed its warmth now. The blood had begun pounding in her veins, and she was sure she must be radiating heat like a furnace. She chuckled to herself. Wasn't that just like a man to blame the woman because he was the one who had sex on the brain.

"You're supposed to be the professional around here," she told him in a tone of voice that tried for indignation but ended up sounding amused. "You're the one Uncle Elvie called on to help find his treasure because he thought you knew all about climbing around in the rocks. This wasn't my idea."

"I know, I know. But I'm sure you'll be the first one smiling when it comes time to split the reward."

She stared at him in mild surprise. "I didn't do it for the money, I did it for Elvie," she replied, stung at the thought that he was accusing her of such a mercenary motive.

"That was part of it, but you were still hoping you might end up with enough cash to fly you back to your precious Paris."

"So what? Then you'll be rid of me."

"That's just the point," he growled. "I don't want to be rid of you."

Her mouth clicked shut and her throat tightened. Of course, he only meant that he wanted her around for the rest of the summer so he could have the hot affair he had previously requested, but it still felt good to hear him admit even that much. "I'm not going anywhere for a while, Deke," she said softly.

"Sure. He stood up, stomping his feet to settle them in his boots before hunkering down to rummage through the pile of equipment that lay next to his backpack.

"I'm going to see this thing through, just the way you are."

"You've got that part right," he muttered.

She raised her eyebrows in mild surprise at his vehement tone but decided not to comment further. Obviously he needed coffee in the morning even more than she did. She gratefully accepted the cup he poured for her, sinking down on the still-rumpled sleeping bags to sip it, being careful not to burn her mouth, which was still in a tender condition from a night spent kissing Deke. The secret awareness sent a thrill of arousal through her.

After breakfast, she followed his lead in getting ready to leave the cave, piling her things neatly off to one side, silently taking her sleeping bag from him after he'd unzipped it from his. Now she understood more clearly why people always called it the cold, cruel light of day. Deke had abruptly returned to a businesslike attitude, and after the closeness they had shared she could only perceive it as a deliberate action to put distance between them.

Reality had taken on a colder, sharper aspect this morning, and although she didn't like it, she realized there was nothing she could do about it. The fusing of their bodies in the dark had seemed so simple, so basic and uncomplicated. She still wanted to revel in it, but Deke had other ideas. It made her want to cry over the loss of her innocent faith that things had to work out because of that fragile bond.

"Are you ready?" he asked. He held out a hand to help her to her feet, squeezing her fingers gently before he released them.

She smiled at the gesture, a soft tilting up of one side of her mouth. "Yes."

"Then let's get out of here and head back to camp. I couldn't see much last night when I grabbed the things we needed, but it wasn't the most opportune time to hang around and check it out. Maybe the person who cut our cord left some kind of calling card."

Deke helped her descend the rocky face of the hill, and then they traveled the now-familiar path back to their campsite. Carly felt like a pro with her newly acquired agility in dealing with such obstacles. She tried hard to ignore the tenderness of her breasts and the soreness between her thighs, but it was difficult when every step reminded her of how their bodies had surged together in that eternal search for completion. She wondered if Deke remembered it too or if he had been able to push it from his mind. Probably the latter, she thought sourly. Men often seemed to have a knack for keeping themselves occupied in the present without dwelling on uncomfortable situations from the past.

When they reached camp they saw that her backpack lay upended with some of its contents spilled out over the grass. "Someone was looking for something, all right," Deke said darkly. "See if anything's missing."

She checked over the small assortment of clothes and other personal items. As she searched, Deke prowled around the area, occasionally bending down to check the ground.

"Everything seems to be here," she told him. "Except for the diary, and you took that along with us into the cave yesterday." She paused, biting her lip thoughtfully. "Wait a minute! That framed photograph of Jesse James that Uncle Elvie gave me is gone." She rummaged through the pack again, but the picture was definitely missing. "Who would want something like that?"

"Someone who's a big fan of Jesse James," Deke said as he got up from the squatting position he'd been in and tossed a clump of dirt to the ground. "Someone who wanted another picture to add to his collection of Jesse memorabilia."

Carly stared at him. "You sound like you have someone in mind."

"I hope I'm wrong about this." He wiped his hand on the back of his jeans. "There are horse tracks over here. From a single animal. I'm going to follow them."

"Not without me!" she cried quickly.

"No, I want you to stay here, Carly."

"No way!" She ran over to clutch at his arm. "I'm not staying here alone. Suppose the person circles around and comes back? Suppose he never left in the first place and is just waiting in those hills somewhere to jump me after you leave? He was mean and ruthless enough to cut our rope and leave us stranded in that horrible pitch-black tunnel. Who knows what he'll do next!"

Deke slipped his arm around her. "All right, you can come. I just thought you might like to rest awhile. After last night," he added meaningfully.

"Oh." A hot flush rippled over her skin beneath the heavy sweater. "No, I'm fine."

"Good." He touched her cheek in a soft, caressing gesture before he stepped away from her. "You don't need to bring anything. I'll carry the field bag. I think we'd better keep that diary with us at all times from now on."

They set off to follow the trail. It was easy to see which way the horse had gone, especially at first where the grassy slope was cut up by the animal's hooves. After that it grew more difficult, although when Deke pointed out broken branches and bent weeds, it became much clearer.

After an hour they came to a ridge that overlooked a small valley. Deke pulled Carly down to the ground and they crawled to the top. Ahead, through a brace of sycamore trees Carly could see a ramshackle house set a good distance back from a two-lane country road. It didn't appear that anyone was living in it until Deke indicated the trail of wispy smoke coming out of the chimney at the side of the house. A nondescript brown horse with a patchy coat grazed in a small, fenced-in pasture.

"This is it," Deke said.

"Do you know who lives there?"

He only nodded, so she poked him impatiently in the ribs. "Who is it?" she hissed.

"Artie Wilkey."

"Oh." She noticed that the roof was badly in need of repair. "Is that good or bad?"

"It could be worse."

"What do we do now?"

"We pay a visit." He grabbed her, pulling her back down when she would have risen to her feet. "Let's approach from the road."

They crept down along the ridge until they came to the pavement, then walked along the side of it until they came to the turnoff for Artie Wilkey's house. Not a single car passed them. Deke pointed to the battered sign at the edge of the driveway.

"There's your culprit."

Carly gasped in surprise when she read the faded black letters. Artie's Country Store. Best Preserves in the Ozarks. Next to that stood another sign, this one more recenty touched up if the faintly darker paint was anything to go by. Outlaw Jesse James Museum, it stated. The next line didn't mince words but went directly to the point, proudly inviting the public to See the Bullet that Done Him In.

Deke took her by the hand, tugging at her arm until she started walking down the gravel drive.

"Business doesn't look very brisk," she commented. She checked up and down the road and in all the other possible directions, but she didn't see any signs of human life.

"I don't think it ever was."

Carly looked at him in amazement, but before she could say anything a woman stepped out onto the front porch. As they approached, Carly could see that she was an older woman, rather heavyset and probably in her sixties. In spite of the chill still hovering in the air, she was neatly dressed in crisp, new Bermuda shorts topped with a matching plaid sleeveless blouse. Curly gray hair formed a halo around her face, which now beamed with a welcoming smile. Carly decided this must be Artie Wilkey's wife or perhaps his mother. Someone devoted to the scoundrel, anyway, for who else would consent to live out here in the middle of nowhere in what practically amounted to a tar-paper shack.

"Hello, folks," she said in a gravelly voice filled to bursting with a thick Missouri twang. "Mighty nice day out today."

Deke nodded politely. "Sure is."

"You come to see the museum?"

"Well, actually no..." Carly began, but Deke jerked on her hand and she quickly stopped.

"Yes, we have. Are you open for business?"

She bobbed her head vigorously. "Sure am, sure am. Right this way, folks." She came down the steps, looking them over as though they were a couple of prize cattle at the state fair. Her expression suddenly turned shrewd. "It's two dollars apiece to get in. Inflation and all being what it is."

Deke reached into his pocket and pulled out his wallet, extracting the money and handing it to her. They followed the woman across the front yard and through the side door of an old garage. A sign above the doorjamb identified the building as the Jesse James Museum.

The old woman flicked on a light switch as she entered the room. Carly's nostrils were assailed with the unmistakable smell of moldy, rotting wood along with a good dose of dust and plain, old-fashioned dirt. She didn't think anyone had even set foot in the place since Jesse James's time, never mind the present century. It was impossible not to cough, although the woman seemed impervious to the thick gloom.

"Haven't had the place open since last summer. I do all my business in the summer, you know."

She strode across to the lone window and threw it open, letting in sunlight and fresh air, although Carly was too far away to draw any immediate benefit from it. Instead, she tried to ignore her tickly throat and glanced at her surroundings.

There wasn't much to see. In the far corner sat an old tractor, once red but now faded to a brownish rust color. All the visible metal parts were rusted, and the leather seat was in tatters and covered with dust and cobwebs. As useless as it was, it took up almost half the interior space of the garage.

"Don't mind that old thing," the woman said, dismissing the ancient contraption with an airy wave of her blue-veined hand. "I'm planning on moving it out of here real soon so's I can expand the museum."

"How nice," Carly responded, smiling, shrugging at Deke.

"Now this here half of the building is the museum proper. Go ahead, help yourselves and look around. If you have any questions, just fire away."

Carly waited for a clue from Deke as to their next move, but he simply walked to the side wall where a table held various items. Everything looked brown and dusty to her eyes, but she followed him to get her two dollars' worth. Personally she was beginning to suspect it was a rip-off.

The trestle table was filled with old newspaper clippings relating to the robberies of the James gang. Some of them were under glass plates and others were simply pasted onto thick vellum pages and propped up on small easels. She thought they might be quite interesting if a person took the time to read them, but her mind was busy trying to figure out what was going on. Deke was no help at all; every time she caught his eye he smiled at her and winked. She supposed if he didn't think they were in any danger, she should just relax.

"This here's a warrant for the arrest of Jesse, issued by the state of Missouri," she said, pointing proudly to a dog-eared, brown-edged paper pressed between two pieces of glass like a dead butterfly. "And this one is issued by the state of Kansas."

"How interesting," Carly murmured when Deke remained silent.

"And here's a company muster roll from the Tennessee Infantry Volunteers listing one J. W. James as AWOL. Actually, that wasn't Jesse James the outlaw, but it's still mighty intriguing."

The room grew quiet when no one made any comment to her statement, but that didn't seem to faze her for she quickly filled in the gap. "I'd offer you lemonade and cookies, but the truth is I don't have any. Do you like this outfit?" Their hostess indicated her clothing with a motion of her hand.

Carly tried to restrain her surprise. "Yes, it's very nice."

The woman smoothed the material against her heavy thighs. "I just bought it yesterday. At the Fashion Express over at Poplar Bluff. I guess I used up the grocery money to do it." There was no hint of self-pity in her voice, no bid for sympathy; she was simply stating a fact. She shrugged as she continued, "Good thing my daughter brought me that casserole yesterday afternoon. It's hard for me living alone out here what with Lukas gone."

"Oh." Carly was drawn into it in spite of herself. "Who's Lukas?"

"Lukas Wilkey was my husband," she explained cheerfully. "By the way, I'm Artressa Wilkey."

"Artressa Brown Wilkey?" Carly asked, her eyes wide with shock. She felt more than a little foolish, for she had totally forgotten about the woman Elvie disliked so much. She had just assumed Artie was a man's name.

"One and the same. I never did like the name Artressa, too fussy and formal, but my momma called me by it till the day she died. Soon as I can sell this place I'm gonna move into town to live with my daughter. I sure hope I can get some good money for it," she added wistfully.

"Who's this?" Deke asked, holding up a small, framed photograph. Carly barely managed to stop herself from gasping when she saw that he held the picture that had been stolen from her backpack. It was the only dust-free object in the place.

"That's Jesse James himself," she said, a smile lighting up her face. "He was always having to worry about getting caught by the law so he never did have many photographs of himself taken. This here's one of them." She walked over to stand next to Deke, proudly admiring the picture over his shoulder. "Those James brothers were a crafty pair, no doubt about it. Did you know they used to switch identities? Jesse would wear heels on his boots so's to look taller than Frank, and then they would reverse it and Frank would be taller than Jesse. It kept the law guessing, that's for sure."

"Where did you get this, Mrs. Wilkey?" Deke asked. His tone reflected simple curiosity but Carly knew better.

"Call me Artie, everybody else does." Artressa Brown Wilkey actually giggled like a teenager.

"All right, Artie. This is Carly Riddle and I'm Deke Baxter."

"Deke Baxter! Any relation to Ed and Opal Baxter?"

"Yes, I'm their son."

"Well, I'll be!" She paused, and her brow furrowed thoughtfully. "Didn't they adopt that other little boy from the city?"

"That was me."

Carly had heard rumors as a child that Deke was adopted, but she'd never known for sure if they were true and she'd never been nosy enough to pursue the topic. It helped to explain why Deke had always acted as though he didn't belong in the little rural town of Justice.

"You were going to tell me how you got this picture," he prodded gently.

Artie was eager to talk. "I found it out in the woods just yesterday. It's a good thing I studied up on old Jesse all these years from a book I have, otherwise I might not have known it was him. I was hoping to find more, but you take what you can get. It really adds the finishing touches to this place, though, don't it?"

"Absolutely," Deke replied softly.

She took the picture from his hands and lovingly wiped the edges with her fingertips. "I didn't have a good photo of Jesse before, just copies from books and those awful line drawings from the Wanted posters, and they don't do his handsome features justice at all. This here picture's the real thing."

"Where did you get the other materials you have here?" Deke asked. Carly was beginning to suspect that all was not quite normal with this old lady.

Artie rocked back on her heels, putting her finger to her lips and staring into Jesse James's face as she considered. "Well, my daddy left most everything you see on that table to me when he died back in the sixties. Only thing is he kept it in a big old black trunk." She straightened to her full height. "It was my idea to open the museum. Lukas was against it from the start, but he relented when he saw it didn't interfere none with my housework and the raising of my little girl.''

"I see." Deke's gaze touched Carly's briefly before he returned his attention to Artie. "So you've added things about Jesse James as you went along?"

"Not really. Only twice, actually."

"And once was when you got this photograph, is that right?" Carly asked encouragingly.

The old woman nodded, eager to talk about it. "That's a fact. The other time was when I got a couple of letters from an old friend. He wanted me to have them for the museum, but he was too bashful to say so."

"So you simply took them."

Her smile was childlike with excitement, as though the cleverness of her actions was finally being understood for the first time. "Yessir, I just took them. I told Lukas that I wanted to make sure that future generations would be able to cherish and enjoy them. He understood right away what I meant."

"Where are those letters, Artie? I don't see them on the table."

"I have them in the house 'cause I was reading them last night. But I'll go fetch them if you'll just wait a minute."

She hurried out of the room leaving Deke and Carly to their own devices.

"What do you know that I don't? You're asking that crazy old lady questions as though you know what you're talking about. Have you been here before?"

"No. But I heard about this place of hers from my parents." Deke pulled her away from the window.

"Haven't you ever wondered why Elvie goes crazy every time her name is even mentioned?"

"Sure. I always figured she jilted him in high school or something. Elvie's a great one for holding a grudge."

"It was much more than being jilted. She stole a couple of Jesse James letters from your uncle a long time ago. I guess she was on the lookout for items for her museum and she heard that Elvie's family might have had some connection with the outlaw.

"Anyway, somehow she got ahold of two of the letters Elvie had in his possession, written by Jesse himself, and she absconded with them. The only part that's public record is how he followed her here with a sixteen-gauge shotgun and threatened to blow her head off if she didn't return the letters. She pulled out her husband's double-barreled twelve-gauge, which is a bigger gun, by the way, although no one is sure to this day whether she ever knew how to use it. So Elvie went home in defeat and that was the end of the matter."

"Maybe for her," Carly huffed indignantly. "Elvie never forgot it. She stole those letters just like she stole that photograph from us. With no hint of remorse. In fact, she seemed very proud of her accomplishments."

"She probably is. According to my mother, who heard it from the sheriff's secretary, she has a mental condition, some kind of social perception disorder. She isn't necessarily crazy, she simply has no conception of the consequences of her actions. She lives in and for the moment."

"So she's the one who cut the cord on us?"

He nodded.

"And this so-called psychological condition excuses her behavior? We almost died because of it."

"Well, that's a little extreme. We came out all right. And no, her condition doesn't excuse her behavior, it merely helps to explain why she acted with such callous disregard for our safety—she wanted to delay our exit from the cave, and in her mind, that was the obvious way to achieve it. If she hadn't wanted us to get out at all she would have removed *all* the eyelets and all the cord."

Carly shuddered. "Now that's a truly terrible thought."

"Now that we know the source of the problem, we can prevent it from happening to us in the future."

"Are you kidding? I'm not going back down in that cave while she's on the loose."

"Shhh. Here she comes."

Artie bustled into the room clutching the letters against her stomach. "Here they are, folks, just like I said."

"Thank you, Artie," he replied, turning his warmest smile in her direction. She beamed back at him. "I'm a Jesse James collector myself," he continued smoothly. "And so is my friend, here. Would you mind if we read through these two letters? I promise you we'll be careful."

"Why sure!" She thrust the letters into Deke's hands. "Here."

Carly watched the interchange thoughtfully. This woman was a paradox. In spite of what she knew Artie had done to get those letters from Elvie, the woman still displayed many of the innocent qualities of a child. She obviously thrived on approval, and yet she could rationalize other ruthless actions without a backward glance. She wondered what plan Deke had in mind.

He handed her the letter written on a single sheet while he kept the longer one. "Here, Carly, you look through this."

"Okay." She glanced down at the cramped handwriting then threw him a puzzled glance.

He nodded at her encouragingly. "You never know how simple letters like these may help fill in the little details, adding to the entire picture."

She grinned. "Of course."

She looked down at the salutation. "Dear Josiah," this one began. These were letters that were originally in Elvie's possession, written to his great grandfather by the outlaw himself. They might contain a clue to help them in their search for the money Jesse left to Josiah McConnell. She quickly scanned the contents, just to capture the general idea, but she was soon deflated. All she saw was another boring description of corn cultivation, just like in the pages of the diary.

She sighed, but buckled down to the task of interpreting every word of the lines of cramped, faded handwriting. The bad grammar and misspellings were enough to send any English teacher into hysterics.

"Here's a recipe for soybean fertilizer," she said after a few minutes of reading, trying to inject enthusiasm into her voice. "Isn't that interesting?"

"I always thought so," Artie said, her still-sharp blue eyes shining as she glanced at each of them. "I figure there must be more to it, else why would Jesse

James, an outlaw and a bank robber, be writing about farming and fertilizer and such?''

"That's a good question, Artie," Deke said. "Did you ever come up with an answer?''

"No," was her glum reply. "But if I ever did, I know I'd be able to sell the museum and the rest of this acreage at a good price and move into town with my daughter. I've had offers for the farm, but no one seems much interested in keeping the museum up and running along with it, and I just can't find it in my heart to sell under those conditions.''

"How many acres do you have here?" he asked thoughtfully.

"Hundred and twenty. Good land, too. My Lukas always said so.''

"Listen, I think I might be able to find you a buyer who meets your conditions. But you'll need to loan me your horse.''

Artie didn't even blink at what Carly considered a complete non sequitur. "She's kind of ornery, but you can have her," the older woman immediately offered.

"Good. I also need to hang on to those two letters of Jesse's for a couple of days, as an example of the kind of memorabilia you have here.''

She sighed heavily, but again she didn't hesitate. "If it will help me keep my museum going, I'll do it." She stuck her hands into her pockets as though that gesture might keep her from snatching the letters back. "I know this little collection about Jesse James might not look like much to you, but it's all I have left to dedicate to my daddy's memory. He would've been proud of what I done with it.''

Half an hour later Deke and Carly were waving to Artressa Wilkey from the back of their borrowed horse as they headed for the foothills of the Ozarks. Artie had happily explained that the scrawny animal carried the grand name of Zerelda, Zee for short, in honor of Jesse's wife.

"Can this poor creature handle our combined weights?" Carly asked from her comfortable position behind Deke.

"Probably not for long. We'll get off up ahead, when we're out of sight of the house."

Carly could feel Zee's bony back beneath her; she swore she could even count each of the horse's ribs as she gripped the animal with her thighs. "What'd you want her for in the first place?"

"So Artie couldn't follow us with a pair of scissors and snip any more cord. She might ride to the cave, but she'll never make it there walking. I also didn't want her to know what we're actually doing. If she heard it concerned Jesse James, there's no telling what scheme she might come up with."

"Good thinking. How do you suppose she found us out there, anyway?"

"Probably saw our campfire and came snooping around."

"She must have thought she'd died and gone to heaven when she came across that picture of Jesse James."

Deke chuckled. "Yeah. She never even questioned why someone was camping out with a framed portrait of the outlaw for company. She just snagged it and ran."

They dismounted after several more interminable minutes of the horse's choppy gait. Deke threw his pack with the fresh supplies they had bought from Artie's country store over his shoulder before he grabbed the reins and they continued walking. Even after that short time in the saddle, Carly had to make an effort not to walk bowlegged the first few steps.

"What are you up to, Deke? Do you really think we can figure out that maze of tunnels in the cave?"

"I don't know. It's just a hunch, but I feel it in my gut that something will pan out. Artie's right about those letters, you know. Jesse didn't write them to Josiah McConnell just to pass the time of day. There must be some kind of clue about where he stashed the money."

Carly pondered that a moment. "Why are you so eager to help her? You don't even know her."

"You shouldn't turn your back on people who need help, even if you don't know them. Ed and Opal Baxter didn't. I don't think I ever appreciated that fact enough."

A fleeting spasm of emotion crossed Deke's face. Carly didn't know much about his early years, and she certainly knew nothing of how he'd spent the time since he'd left Justice, but she was beginning to realize that his life hadn't been easy or even particularly blessed the way hers had been. She decided to help him change the subject.

"Hey, you know what?" she asked with a cheeky grin, peering around Zee's bobbing head so she could look directly at Deke. "We never even got to see the Bullet That Done Him In!"

"IT SURE WOULD BE NICE if we had a map of the cave," Carly said. She leaned back against the tree, where she had propped the sleeping bag Deke had retrieved from the mouth of the cavern an hour earlier when they had first begun searching the diary and the letters for clues. Zerelda grazed peacefully nearby.

"Dream on, Carly." Deke didn't look up from the pages he was reading for what had to be the third time.

"It's not all that farfetched. After all, there are several maps in that diary, those farmer's diagrams of which fields were planted with which crops."

Deke grunted. "What we need is a written description like the one we used to find the cave."

"That would be nice, too."

She slid a little farther down along the tree trunk, drowsy in the warmth of the afternoon sun. Her night of lovemaking with Deke was finally catching up with her, and the sensation of tired accomplishment she was experiencing was extremely pleasant. She was finding it hard to concentrate on much of anything, although he didn't seem to be having the same problem. She wondered if he had thought about their lovemaking the way she had and if he too was curious about what the night would bring.

"This one isn't a map of crops," he said, stabbing a finger at one of the pages. "It's a map of Justice."

"Oh, yes, I remember it." She shrugged lazily. "When I first saw it I thought the mapmaker had a pretty skewed concept of perspective, but then again, who knows what Justice looked like in those days."

"It looked basically the way it does now." Deke's voice held a puzzled note in it that caught her attention.

"You're right," she said, sitting up straighter. "Let me see those letters again." She held out her hand, waiting patiently as he set the diary down before handing her the letters. "There's a line here somewhere about the streets of Justice...." She ran her finger down the page until she found the reference. "Here it is, in the middle of a paragraph about planting a garden. 'Keep the rows of vegetables straight and true like the streets of Justice, which, if you carefully check your map, are laid out in a gridiron.'"

Deke frowned. "That doesn't make any sense."

"Yes it does." Her voice quivered with excitement as she scooped the diary from the ground and opened it to the map in question. "Don't you see? This map isn't of Justice at all. None of the streets are even labeled, and they certainly don't bear any resemblance to a gridiron. A gridiron contains parallel lines and squares. There's not a single ninety-degree angle anywhere on the page."

He scooted over next to her while she pointed out what she had previously thought to be the edge of town. "Look, this must be the entrance to the cave. And here are those two main arteries. Deke, this is it! We found the map showing the configuration of the tunnels!"

Chapter Eight

Deke helped Carly up to the cave entrance before tying a rope around the crowbar and pry bar he had brought along so he could drag them up to the mouth of Jesse's cave. She had never seen anything like the pry bar, a thick, five-foot length of steel that Deke assured her might come in handy if they had to pry any boulders loose. She hadn't forgotten the sight of it hanging across Deke's back like an Indian bow that first day on the trail.

His voice now brought her back to the present. "We'll leave this stuff here for now." He nodded at the floor of the cave toward the equipment, which lay in an undignified heap where he had tossed it. "We might not need it, and I don't want to drag all that heavy steel down a passage until I have to. Now, where's the map?"

"Right here." She handed him the diary, which had a marker to indicate the page. She watched as he flipped it open and began studying it.

After five minutes of intensive perusal he snapped it shut. "I think I've got it. We came pretty close the second day we were in here, but according to this we missed a passage that opens off the main one about halfway along.''

They started down the second of the tunnels that led off the cavern. Deke seemed to know exactly where he was going, only stopping to verify his direction when they came to a crossroad. Soon they entered a long, straight passage that Carly recognized from the angel-hair formations and calcite-covered walls as one where they'd been before. She also thought she remembered that it had stopped abruptly in a dead end, and sure enough, they came to a solid wall of limestone and could go no farther.

''This is it,'' Deke said, sounding excited.

Carly was more skeptical. ''How do you know?'' she asked. ''I don't see any hidden passages.''

Deke tugged her to one side and then began pacing back from the rock wall. When he reached a certain point, he stopped. ''Right here.''

He began feeling along the wall for a moment before he called, ''Come and shine your light over here, Carly.''

She did as he requested, pointing her beam of light along the boulder-strewn wall. ''Don't tell me it's behind one of these monsters?'' she said grimly. The boulders were almost as tall as she was and certainly much wider. She didn't think the two of them together could even begin to budge them if that's what he had in mind.

Deke was now crawling along the top of the largest rock, poking his fingers into the cracks around its edges and grunting as though he were talking to the inanimate behemoth and it was answering. He pointed the beam of light along the top. ''Oh, yeah, baby,'' he crooned, patting the rock fondly. "Carly, look at this."

She made a face but immediately began to scramble past the loose rocks along the wall to where he was located. He pulled her up the last couple of yards. "Look over there," he instructed, pointing upward. "I'll hold your light."

He aimed both flashlights at a spot on top of the boulder, and Carly gasped when she saw the faint writing there. Scratched right into the rock were a series of symbols like the ones in the corner of the original map. "Oh, neat," she cried excitedly. Then her expression faltered and she frowned. "Oh, no. Does that mean we have to move this thing out of the way?"

"Exactly," he said with satisfaction.

"You don't need to look so pleased about it."

"Why not? I am pleased about it. I intend to take out my frustrations on that obstructive piece of cave real estate."

She wasn't immune to the meaningful look he was aiming at the curve of her hips and down along the seat of her jeans. That, and the flush that warmed her body in instant response, made her realize that her pose on the rocks above him was rather provocative if your thoughts happened to run in that direction. Obviously his did, and it didn't take much to lure hers away from treasure and directly onto the same wavelength.

"Well, don't let me stop you," she said tartly.

"You're the one who started me." He jumped directly off the wall to the floor of the passage, landing as gracefully as a cat, then held up his hand to her. "Come on down from there."

Her descent was less artistic. She slid down using her hands and feet as brakes. Nevertheless, she managed to get up enough speed so that she landed against Deke's chest with a whooshing sound. He caught her in his arms, his hands immediately going to her hips before slipping down and around to the real objects of his quest, pulling her tighter against him so that she could feel his arousal. The thought that she could inspire such instant and obvious desire melted her reserve.

When she looked up into his face, he quickly bent down to kiss her. It was a gentle little kiss, especially considering their physical state. He pulled away just as she was heating up.

"Save some of that for later tonight," he said, drawing in a deep, steadying breath. His hand brushed her cheek as his gaze roved over her face, his eyes alight with amusement. "I don't think I'll push my luck by trying for a bout of lovemaking on the floor of this cave."

She smiled in quick response, quirking her brows as she looked around the passageway. She was honest enough to admit to herself that she'd momentarily forgotten where they were. She was also surprised at the sharp stab of disappointment she was experiencing because he hadn't even tried to push past what he thought were her reservations. She wondered how she would have responded to such unembellished passion in this elemental setting.

He grinned crookedly as he gently pushed her away. "Right now, I'd better get my mind off sex and back onto the business at hand. Do you want to wait here while I go back for the pry bar? I'll only be a few minutes."

"I guess so," she said.

"Okay, I'll be right back."

She watched him head down the passageway, his ground-eating strides quickly delivering him to where the tunnel took a sharp right around a smooth outcropping of stone. His light disappeared around the corner, leaving her only the illumination of her own. She sat down on a small boulder across from the one he intended to move and contemplated what would happen if and when they actually found some money.

"Deke will return to South America again, and you'll be off to Paris, where you belong," she whispered out loud. Her voice sounded small and hollow in the enclosed space. The thrill she usually got from that thought was dampened by the ties she'd begun forging with Deke, in spite of the fact that she knew they were temporary. Women fell for it every time, and in this situation she was no different from the rest of her gender. Just like Deke, she wasn't about to let a summer affair interfere with plans that she'd made before all this had even begun. She hadn't forgotten the life she had carved out for herself in Paris, and yet she found herself wanting to stick around Justice and pursue this thing with Deke, to follow him to the ends of the earth, to have her cake and eat it, too.

She frowned at the boulder, hoping this didn't mean she was in love with him or anything fatal like that. She squeezed her eyes shut, trying to visualize the elegant crowds of Paris on their way to attend the theater, but nothing was going right for her today. In place of suave, sophisticated, dark-haired chevaliers, her mind stubbornly produced a blond, Missouri-drawling rogue who didn't know the Comédie-Française from the Three Stooges.

If nothing else, when the time came for them to part and Deke returned to his wayward life, waving good-bye to her without a backward glance as she half suspected would be the case, she would at least be able to do the same.

To take her mind off a subject that had no solution because it wasn't even yet a problem, she turned off her flashlight, hoping to distract herself. The effect was enough to make her gasp in fright as she got a real taste of how deep inside the earth she really was.

Was this how it would have been yesterday if they hadn't found the way out? Without any light, the dark was so thick, so encompassing, that it was almost a malevolent, living presence. Her sense of perspective was totally skewed, and sweat broke out on her upper lip when she realized that the air suddenly seemed thick and unbreathable.

She quickly snapped the flashlight back on, moaning in fervid relief when the walls and floor of the passage came back into focus around her. Her heart was pounding so hard, she seriously thought she might have a heart attack. When she heard the sounds of Deke approaching, she giggled to herself, trying not to notice the note of hysteria creeping into her tone. Well, she had certainly gotten her mind off the subject of her and Deke.

"How long are these batteries good for?" she asked him as soon as she could see his face. "Did you bring any extras today?"

He dumped the equipment at her feet, tilting his head to gaze up at her. He must have seen some remnants of her battle with the dark in her eyes because he straightened to his full height and reached for her hand. "What'd you do, turn off your light?"

"How did you know?"

"You have the same expression on your face that I've seen on people who have been lost in the jungle for a few days. Like they didn't quite realize what it was really going to be like."

"I never knew the dark could be so total and so unforgiving."

"Yeah, it's quite an experience. To answer your question, I've got spare batteries, and the ones already in there are good for five hours of use, so you've got a ways to go before you get stranded in the dark. After yesterday's little episode, I've become even more careful, believe me. And this time I've chiseled a mark beside each eyelet so we can follow them back to the mouth of the cave whether there's any cord there or not."

She smiled weakly. "Thanks for not making fun of me."

"I never make fun of the awesomeness of nature or the vagaries of chance. That would be asking for trouble, and I don't need any more of that than I've already had."

She helped him clear the area around the boulder and then stepped back to watch as he maneuvered the pry bar underneath the massive structure.

"Using the law of leverage I should be able to move a couple of tons. Let's hope that this boulder doesn't weigh any more than that." He grunted as he tested the bar's positioning. "Besides, I only have to roll it enough so that we can squeeze past it."

He groaned as he put his full weight behind his efforts. Carly could see the tendons in his neck standing out with the strain as he gritted his teeth. His back and shoulder muscles strained beneath the material of his shirt, and she could feel her heart pounding faster in sympathy, as though that would help boost his blood's circulation and increase his strength. The boulder didn't budge.

He frowned as he studied the situation again, moving the pry bar to a slightly different position against the boulder before taking up his stance beside it once more. This time when he pushed, she heard a scraping sound as the boulder creaked forward before falling back into the groove it had been cradled in all these years.

"That's it," Deke grunted, attacking the bar again. With a series of jerky motions he rocked the boulder little by little to one side until Carly actually saw that there was a passage behind it. She quickly pointed her flashlight into the opening.

"Can you see anything?" he asked.

"A tunnel." As she leaned forward to peer into it, she could feel a gust of cool air against her face. "It looks like all the others we've been through."

"Good."

He groaned and heaved and sweated as he caused the huge rock to slide, inch by inch, until the opening became somewhat larger. Carly didn't think a dog could fit through it, but she kindly refrained from pointing that out, not wanting to deflate Deke after all his efforts.

"That ought to do it."

"You've got to be kidding," she breathed in dismay. "I can't fit through there."

"Sure you can," he said with a grin, eyeing her slim figure and holding up his hands as though measuring her, comparing their dimensions to the opening. "And I should know." He quirked a roguish eyebrow in her direction. "Better not get me started on that again."

"All right. But you go first."

"Sure." He wedged the pry bar along the opening, insuring that they would be able to use it from inside the newly discovered passage in case the rock somehow rolled back into place and trapped them. "See, I'm not taking any chances," he told her. Then he squeezed himself and his flashlight through the narrow opening until he disappeared.

Carly peered in.

"It's another one of those huge caverns." His voice was filled with excitement. "And Carly, I see a trunk over against the far wall."

"Wait for me," she cried. Taking a deep breath and clearing her mind of all the logical reasons why a human body wouldn't make it through, even though she had just seen Deke do it, she pushed herself into the opening, feeling only a moment of panic before she was free from the claustrophobic embrace of rock wall and boulder.

Deke was waiting for her. "It looks like we've found it," he said.

They crossed the floor of the cavern. This room wasn't as large as the master cave, but it was impressive nonetheless. Masses of stalactites hung from the ceiling where they were met in some places by stalagmites rising from the floor. Some of the iciclelike formations had been broken off, whether by gravity or by human hands, it was hard to tell. The overall color of both rocks and floor was a rusty brown with both lighter and darker veins of various minerals running through some of the larger planes of the wall.

They approached the trunk cautiously, as though they expected Dracula to rise out of its massive depths and greet them with a cheery, heavily accented "Good evening." Carly had never seen such a large piece of luggage. Not even a steamer trunk could approach it in size. The top was fastened with a heavy metal hasp, but luckily there was no padlock dangling from its swivel eyelet to protect the contents, so they wouldn't have to break into it by force.

Deke ran his fingers respectfully along the lid. He looked at her and she nodded, reaching out to grasp his arm with both hands as she watched him open the lid. They both bent to stare into its dark depths.

"What in the world...? It looks like a bunch of photographs," Carly said, wrinkling her brow as her mind tried to absorb what her eyes were seeing. The inside of the trunk was not even filled halfway but unless there was a pile of money underneath all the photos, it didn't look like they'd be going home wealthy.

Deke reached down and grabbed a handful of the old, sepia-toned pictures and began to go through them. "Look at this," he said, his voice filled with amazement. "They're all of Jesse James."

"Why do you sound so surprised? We knew we were looking for his bank stash, why not other things of his as well?"

"Don't you remember how Artie said that he never allowed anyone to take any photos of him? He said he didn't want people to be able to recognize him so they could report on his whereabouts and turn him in. Not that it helped him in the end, since it was one of his own supposed friends who shot him in the back for the reward."

She shot him a surprised look and he shrugged. "Everybody knows that. Just ask Elvie."

Carly had only seen that one picture of the outlaw, but she was sure getting a taste of every nuance of the man's facial structure now that Deke held out picture after picture of Jesse James for her inspection. Most of them were the stiff, formal photos so common in that era, like the one of Jesse sitting on a straight-backed chair, his hat in his hands as he stared at the camera, looking for all the world as though he were about to attend a funeral. Some of the pictures showed him alone and some had him posed with various members of his gang, and there were almost a dozen shots of him with a woman who had to be his mother. He wasn't a handsome man exactly, but she could see that there was something appealing about him. In fact he reminded her a little of Deke.

Her attention was especially caught by one photo of him posed in front of what looked like an outhouse, a grin lighting up his ascetic features. How young he looked in that one, she thought. A strand of his dark hair hung down over one eye and his clothes seemed too big for his thin body, but his boyish charm and sense of fun were evident in the way he held his hand threateningly over the door handle as though to open it and expose the occupant. The air of authority he showed when photographed with his gang was absent from this picture, and she felt a trace of sadness that he had turned to a life of crime.

"I wonder why he took all these pictures," Carly mused.

Deke shrugged. "Maybe he made a deal with the McConnells to sell them to the newspapers after his death so he could go on being famous. I'm sure he didn't figure he would live to a ripe, old age, and this was his stab at immortality."

"That's possible." Carly tapped the corner of one picture against her chin thoughtfully. "But I'd rather believe that he had these taken for his wife and kids so they wouldn't forget what he looked like after he was gone."

"Don't forget that the man was a robber and a cold-blooded killer. He wasn't exactly a nice guy, Carly."

She shrugged off his assessment. "I've read that he often helped the poor."

"Oh right, Jesse James, Missouri's version of Robin Hood. I hate to point this out, but those stories are completely unsubstantiated. Some of the facts about his life may have been in doubt, but everyone knows he wasn't a Good Samaritan."

"Well, he left his money to the McConnells in return for a favor, didn't he? He didn't have to do that." Her thoughts returned to the photos and she knew she was right. "Besides, he obviously loved his mother so he couldn't have been all bad."

Deke shook his head and laughed. "I'm not about to argue with feminine logic."

They glanced through the remaining pictures all the way to the bottom of the trunk. "This is all very nice, and I'm sure Artie would sell her soul to get her hands on all these photographs for her museum," Deke commented, looking over his shoulder at her, "but it's not the fortune Elvie was dreaming of. I wonder what happened to the money."

"Maybe this will explain." She held out a stack of little pieces of paper that had been clipped together.

Deke looked down at the top sheet. "What is it?"

"A stack of IOUs. It looks like some of Elvie's relatives have been here before us."

"You're kidding." He looked down at the faded handwriting and began to read. "'I, Daniel McConnell, am taking the last of the money left to Josiah McConnell by Jesse James, outlaw, to pay the taxes on my farm.' It's signed and dated 1932."

Carly nodded. "It must have been during the Depression. No one had any ready cash back then. Uncle Elvie was always telling me stories about how his grandfather owned hundreds of acres in Arkansas and how he had to sell them off during the Depression just so he and his family could survive."

"Nice of him to let us know what happened to everything." He flipped through the rest of the papers. "They've been dipping into the money practically since the day it was left here." He made a sound of disgust. "I don't know why they bothered to leave those IOUs when they never intended to pay it back."

"Well, at least they were honorable and only took what they needed." She grinned, thumbing through the dozen or so pieces of paper that comprised the stack. "As far as I can tell at least three generations got their hands on some of that money. And they only used it for their farms, not to go out and have a wild time.''

"What a comfort.'' Deke began returning the photos to the trunk. "I'd love to hand these pictures over to Artie. They're of no use to Elvie, but I guess it's up to him what he wants to do with them.''

Carly bit her lip. "I doubt he'd ever let her have them. You heard how he reacted when you mentioned her name the other day.''

"Then we'd better leave the trunk here for now.''

"Right.''

Carly brushed off a small, stone slab and sat down on it. She watched Deke close the lid of the trunk before idly swinging her light around the room. She wasn't searching for anything in particular, but their quest had come to such a dead halt and in her mind it still seemed unfinished. Probably that was because her relationship with Deke was heading for the same brick wall. She wondered if once their adventure was over she would even see him again. And to top off that cheerful thought, here they were, the proud possessors of an unexplained trunkful of photos of a dead outlaw who didn't like having his picture taken.

She didn't really know what she expected to find, but she could feel herself becoming obsessed about covering the entire wall surface of this inner cavern with the beam of her flashlight. She didn't stop to try to figure out what was driving her, she simply followed her instincts.

This particular room had no other tunnels or passageways leading off it, although over on the far wall opposite Jesse's trunk was a small alcove, almost like a grotto where a statue should be standing. Even the stone seemed to be made of a different material, being somewhat smoother and shinier than the rest of the rock surrounding it.

She walked over to investigate, running her fingers across the surface. Looking to her left, she was surprised to discover that the recessed wall acted as a blind and that behind it lay a narrow passageway that seemed to squeeze around the rock wall that formed the alcove. It didn't look as though it actually went anywhere, and she quickly estimated that a normal-sized human being would have to plaster himself against the rock if he even wanted to try, but she knew that wouldn't stop Deke.

She stepped back, shining her light above the little grotto, half expecting to see some kind of inscription, like the ones decorating the catacombs in Rome. When she saw the simple but stylized line drawing of a turtle, its elongated neck and head pointing straight down at where her feet were planted, she gasped.

"Deke, look what I've found."

When he didn't answer she glanced back to find that he was staring at the turtle in awe. "That's the symbol the Spanish used to indicate where they'd hidden their silver and gold," he said. Then he whooped. "Carly, you just might become a rich woman yet!"

"There's an opening at the back of that alcove, but it's not big enough to fit through," Carly told him. She leaned against the rock wall, watching Deke explore the area, careful not to touch any part of her bare flesh against the cold, damp stone.

He grunted in what she assumed was a reply as he checked along the back wall. Part of him disappeared as he tried to wedge his body into the narrow passage without success. He stared at the rock for several long moments and then she saw him slip out of his jacket.

"This wall has been moved by a fairly recent earthquake," he called back to her. "I'm going to see where it leads."

"Deke, no!" Her stomach clenched in panic at the thought of Deke's hard, muscled body trying to push and mold itself to the inhumanly narrow confines of that passageway. "Don't be crazy. You're going to get stuck in there before you go two feet."

He peered back around the corner of the rock, grinning at her. "If that's the case, then you shouldn't have any trouble yanking me back out."

"Is that before or after I get hysterical?" she retorted hotly.

"Would you really get hysterical over me, Carly?" Even in the fluctuating light she could tell that his blue eyes crinkled with amusement. "I'm flattered."

"Cut it out, Deke, this isn't funny," she cried, crossing her arms over her chest to contain her emotions and to keep herself from lashing out at him in fear and frustration. Visions of the body she had caressed and loved only hours before caught between jagged edges of unyielding rock, his shirt ripped, his flesh torn and bleeding, flashed through her mind.

"You might get hurt," she whispered.

He crossed the cave floor to where she stood, taking her into his arms and holding her close. She clung to him as though they were the last two people on earth. "Carly, sweetheart, don't be upset. I know what I'm doing. I've been through fissures and crevices even smaller than this one. Lots of times. At least if I make a mistake, I won't plunge hundreds of feet to my death like I would on some South American altiplano."

"Oh, great. Is that supposed to make me feel better?"

His hands, which had been stroking her back in a comforting motion, suddenly dipped down below her hips to the seat of her jeans.

"How can you think about sex at a time like this?" she wailed.

He gripped her by the waist, leaning back so he could look at her, shaking his head in wry self-amusement. "I seem to be thinking about it all the time, lately. And that was even before last night happened." The amusement fled from his gaze. "The real experience knocked everything I had imagined right out of the ballpark."

He bent down to gently kiss her on the mouth. It happened so quickly that her eyes had only just drifted closed before it was over. She opened them again to find him smiling down at her. She had never seen such a soft expression on his face or in his eyes.

"Don't worry, Carly. I'm not going to do anything foolish."

She sighed. "Okay."

She watched him retrace his steps back to the alcove, and before she knew it, he had again disappeared behind the wall of rock like the White Rabbit slipping down the rabbit hole. Only she wasn't Alice in Wonderland and she didn't have a magic mushroom to shrink her in size so she could fit through the crevice. She walked over to the place she had last seen him and settled down to wait.

She didn't have to do so very long. She heard Deke shout, and then his excited, disembodied voice carried back to her through the passage in the most eerie fashion, as though he were talking to her from inside a tin can. "Carly, you're not going to believe this. You have to come and see for yourself."

"Over my dead body," she retorted.

"I'm coming back to get you, sweetheart," he shouted cheerfully.

She waited only moments before his hand came into view, then the arm attached to it followed. With a grunt and a nasty shredding noise, he popped out from the crevice like a piece of bread from a toaster.

"Carly," he said breathlessly. His eyes were shining with excitement, his motor running on high speed. Hers was too, only for a different reason, namely stark terror. "You have to see it. I'm not going to tell you what's on the other side of that wall because you have to see it for yourself."

Her smile was tight. "No thanks."

"It looks like a closer fit than it really is, honest, Carly. After the first yard it opens out so that you have at least half an inch to spare. And I'm bigger than you." He grabbed her arm and spun her around to look at him. "Look, I wouldn't ask you to do it if I thought there was any danger. We're partners, and partners trust each other."

She didn't answer because her throat was working convulsively and she couldn't utter a sound.

"Please believe me, Carly, when I tell you that this is the find of a lifetime. I didn't even explore very thoroughly because we should do it together."

What could she say when he pleaded so eloquently? How could she refuse him? She was in over her head, and she didn't know what else to do but trust him. Besides, she could feel the adrenaline beginning to shoot through her veins as she wondered what he had seen on the other side of the passage.

"All right. I'll try. But if I get scared, I'm turning back."

"I'll be right there with you, sweetheart. You just have to do what I do."

"Okay. Let's go before I chicken out."

She followed him to the alcove, her heart thundering in her ears. She could feel a light sheen of perspiration beginning to form on her body, and yet she felt chilled to the bone.

"Should I take off my jacket?" she asked. Her voice sounded tinny and small to her own ears.

"Nah. You're slim enough to make it through without doing that."

Taking great gulps of oxygen, hoping to store away a reserve supply of it in case she got squeezed in too tight for breathing, she watched Deke stretch out his arms until he was holding the boulder like a lover. Then he began to inch his way around its pockmarked side.

"See, it's easy," he called back to her over his shoulder. "Just grab my hand and I'll help pull you through. Think about something pleasant and you'll be on the other side before you know it."

She couldn't see any part of him now except his left wrist and the hand that was groping for hers. With a deep breath she placed hers in it and closed her eyes.

Every muscle was screaming in protest, but she inched her way forward, each step bringing her body into closer contact with the clammy rock that tugged and prodded at the material of her jacket. It pressed closer and closer until finally her breasts were flattened and every inch of her back felt the cool stone wall against it. And still Deke tugged on her arm.

"I'm stuck," she said. She was utterly calm now, knowing that her fate was sealed forever and that they would find her years from now, her skeleton still clutching the rock in an eternal embrace.

"No you're not," Deke countered, giving a last sharp tug. She screamed as the resistance that had been holding her back gave way and she felt herself falling through empty space. Luckily Deke was there to catch her before she hit the floor.

"Oomph" was all she could manage in a breathless voice. She was too busy grabbing his arms, his shirt, whatever was within reach. Her eyes had flown open in her final terror, but they still weren't focusing very well. Even Deke's smiling face appeared hazy and unclear.

"Go on," he urged her. "Take a look around."

Carly cried out in surprise as her startled gaze took in the walls and ceiling. Alice in Wonderland was an appropriate metaphor, after all. It certainly looked as though she had wandered into some kind of fairyland, she thought, as an entire spectrum of colors was reflected back at her from the beam of her flashlight. Undulating bands of silver, white and an otherworldly blue glistened along the far wall as they were illuminated in turn. She half expected to see a pack of gossamer-winged fairies waving their little wands and trailing rainbows behind them.

"What is this stuff?" she breathed in awe.

"Onyx. It's a form of agate, a semi-precious stone."

She continued to stare until Deke's light picked out a formation in the far corner that resembled a table and a bench made of the same multihued onyx. "It looks like someone's dining room."

"Yeah. And check what's on the menu for dinner."

This time she didn't gasp or scream. The shock of what she was seeing in the middle of that underground table was beyond the realm of mere vocal sounds. She began to walk toward it, Deke keeping pace right at her side. She automatically reached for his hand.

"Is it silver?" she asked reverently.

"I'm afraid so," he chuckled.

They stopped when they reached the table. There on top of its smooth surface sat a majestic pile of silver ingots, neatly stacked in a pyramidlike shape and looking for all the world like the centerpiece for a fancy dinner party. Carly ran her fingers along the flat plane of stone. It was cool to the touch, like everything else in this cave, but it seemed clean and pure to her, unlike the dirty rock walls and granite boulders. She couldn't bring herself to reach for the silver.

"It must have a curse on it or something. Why else would it be sitting there so brazenly out in the open. You pick it up."

"Thanks a lot." He released her hand. "If you see the floor shake or hear the walls rumble, you'd better start running."

He reached for the top ingot, pulling it carefully away from its brothers and sisters, holding it reverently in both hands. He stroked the surface, then held it out to her.

"No curse yet," he said.

She took it from his hands. The weight surprised her. It was so smooth, so shiny, that she could see the light reflected back from its surface.

"What's one of these worth, do you think?" she asked.

"Last time I looked silver was five dollars an ounce. This baby must weigh somewhere around thirty pounds. So I'd guess almost twenty-five hundred dollars.

"Wow."

Deke began pulling the ingots toward him, stacking them in another pile as he counted them. " . . . Eighteen, nineteen, twenty."

Something wedged in the juncture where the table joined the wall caught her eye, not because it was shiny, but because it wasn't and therefore out of place in the midst of all this smooth stone and silver. She hoisted herself onto the edge of the table and crawled toward it, discovering that it was a dirty-looking brown sack about the size of a bowling ball. She picked it up, grunting in surprise at its weight. She had to place her hand underneath it so she could drag it across the onyx table; whatever was inside was heavy enough to threaten the threadbare cloth that contained it.

"Look, Deke. This feels like a bag full of those fishing weights Elvie uses." She sat on the edge of the table, letting her legs dangle, the bag beside her. She untied the thin piece of rawhide that held the neck of the sack closed and peered inside, ready to jump back. She frowned.

"Well, what is it?" he asked impatiently.

She gingerly reached inside and drew out a handful of the contents, holding them out on the palm of her hand for Deke's inspection. "You tell me."

He looked at her in wonder. "They're bullets, Carly."

"Oh, no," she breathed. "Do you think..."

"That they're Arvil Crook's? It seems a likely possibility, doesn't it?"

He took the bag from her, rummaging around in it before saying, "Yup, it's a bagful of bullets." He dumped all but one back into the sack, taking it in his fingers and holding it up to the light to examine it. It looked rather blackened and pockmarked and not at all like the ingots. "These are definitely homemade bullets, and you know what, Carly?"

She shook her head.

"They're also pure silver."

"Then they are Arvil's."

He grinned. "Who else would be stupid enough to make bullets out of silver in the first place."

"Unless they were trying to kill a vampire." She blew out her breath. "I'm confused. How did Arvil Crook and the Spanish conquistadores end up in the same silver mine? If this is a mine."

"I don't think it is. We haven't seen any evidence of mining activity in this cave, although it might connect to one that does," Deke said slowly. "I'm thinking that maybe they both used this cavern to hide their treasures."

"So did Jesse James," she pointed out.

"Yeah. But it doesn't look like Jesse ever went far enough inside this place to discover the ingots. Supposedly he disliked using caves as hideouts; a posse could too easily track him down and ambush him when he came out. But nobody was on old Arvil's trail. He must have done some exploring and found the ingots."

"Then why didn't he take them with him? Why are they still here?"

"That's the mystery, all right." Deke took a long, last look at the bullet before tossing it into the sack. "It's almost as though he finally realized the value of what he'd thought was his iron mine and came in here to hide the silver bullets. Then he discovered these ingots and stockpiled everything until he could return for it."

"So why didn't he return?"

"I don't know."

Carly glanced from the ingots to the bag of bullets, her expression thoughtful. "Here's my theory about the whole thing. I think Arvil Crook wandered in here one day, obviously being a man who wasn't averse to exploring old mines and caves, and he found the ingots. And that's when he realized that the bullets he had handed out to his neighbors were silver."

"Could be."

She frowned. "But it still doesn't make sense that he never came back for all this. It's worth a fortune."

"According to the story, after his wife died, Crook sent his kids on ahead to relatives in Texas, then packed up the farm and followed them there. Said he wanted to start a new life." Deke reached over to retie the rawhide cord around the neck of the sack, staring at it thoughtfully. ''Just the bullets alone would have set him up for life, never mind the ingots.''

''Something must have happened to him. Either that or these aren't his silver bullets.''

''Well, they're ours now.''

Her eyes sparkled. ''Just wait till Elvie sees this. How can we break it to him gently, without giving him another heart attack?''

''People don't get heart attacks from good shocks.''

''Yes they do.''

''You're right.'' His grin was wicked. ''Now that you mention it, I recall reading in the newspaper just the other day about a seventy-year-old man and his thirty-two-year-old bride. He had a heart attack on his wedding night.''

''That wasn't quite the example I had in mind.''

Deke nodded, continuing with his train of thought, ignoring her good-natured exasperation. ''I can picture it now. She wore French underwear beneath her wedding gown, pure silk straight from Paris. Caused him to keel right over.''

He laughed as she glared at him, then he walked over to where she sat and fitted himself between her knees until he was wedged snugly against the core of her body. Her exasperation fled along with the breath from her lungs.

''Take me, for example,'' he continued softly, pressing forward until she was forced to put her arms around his neck to keep from falling backward. ''I'm a lot younger than seventy and those lacy little scraps of material sure gave me one hell of a jolt.'' His voice lowered to become even more intimate.

She watched his mouth move as he spoke. The melting warmth of his hot gaze acted like a sunlamp on her face; she could feel her cheeks reddening with the blood that was pounding through the rest of her body. His mouth hovered above hers, his warm breath caressing her lips.

"Sweetheart, you make me ache," he said. "I am so hard for you right now that I can't tell anymore whether it's pain or pleasure." He allowed his body to thrust softly against hers to demonstrate the validity of his words, and because her position left her so vulnerable, the movement quickened her nerve endings with the force of an electric power surge. "They may not be the sweet, romantic words you want to hear, but they're the unvarnished truth."

She closed her eyes against the searing heat of his gaze, moaning a little just because she couldn't seem to stop the sound from leaving her mouth. Deke needed no more encouragement than that to push her down until she was lying flat along the top of the onyx table. He quickly reached for the snap of her jeans, wrenching it open in his impatience and pulling the zipper down with a jerk.

His urgency was contagious. Carly had never been possessed by a whirlwind before. It took her breath away and made her as crazy for him as he was for her. She didn't even care that she was deep inside the earth, that the stone beneath her was cold, that the air was moist and smelled of mold. She only knew she wanted Deke inside her more than she wanted words, almost more than she wanted breath in her body.

She watched him through slitted eyes as he ripped his shirt off. She didn't realize what he meant to do until he lifted her and pulled her jeans down her legs then slid the shirt underneath her body to protect her bareness from contact with the stone. That gallant little act melted her heart completely and she reached for him.

For a brief moment she thought about how she must look lying there like that, how wanton and how unlike the image she had always carried around of herself. Then every thought flew out of her head as Deke slid inside her, stroking all her secret places, his body pounding against hers until she cried out to beg him not to stop, knowing that no one could possibly hear her.

It wasn't long before her body convulsed in such deep throes of pleasure that she lost all sense of time and place and the boundaries of their separate beings. Seconds later Deke followed her with a wrenching cry. He held his body deep inside her for long moments then collapsed on top of her with a sigh.

They lay like that until their breathing quieted, then Deke raised himself so he could look down at her. "You must be cold and uncomfortable," he said with tender concern.

He started to move but she clutched at him with weak arms. "No, don't go just yet. I'm all right." Her smile was dreamy. "Believe me, I'm just fine."

She shifted her body a little, slowly becoming aware of her position, of how her legs dangled against the rock and how the onyx pressed into her back. She allowed her hands to roam over Deke's bare shoulders and back, absorbing the smooth texture of his skin and the resilience of his muscles. When she felt the goose bumps rippling his flesh, she struggled to sit up.

"You're the one who's cold," she said, pushing at him until he stood up.

He grinned as he stepped back from her and fastened his jeans. "My mind may say it's cold in here but the rest of me doesn't seem to care where I am." He glanced around the cavern.

"I know what you mean," she said, rubbing the back of her neck with one hand, feeling slightly embarrassed to face him after the way she had totally let herself go. She hadn't envisioned ever experiencing anything like that in her life. She felt exposed and afraid that he had been allowed a glimpse of something she wasn't ready for him to see. She quickly pulled her jeans up over her chilled thighs. "Talk about raw sex," she commented in a light voice.

"Is that what you think this was?"

"Sure." She handed him his shirt then smiled, although it came out a weak effort. She knew she was lying, but it was the only way she could protect herself from sliding into an abyss where there was nothing left of her because she had given it all to Deke. Her vision of how her life should be was dissolving before her very eyes; she had to stop the process now, before she reached the point of no return and ruined everything. "You promised direct and all-American and you delivered it."

His face showed his anger. "How about describing it as honest and sincere, Carly?"

"Now who's talking about semantics?"

"Semantics have nothing to do with it. We're talking about the truth of what just went on here." He glared at her as he shoved his arms into the shirt and pulled it over his head. "And by the way, I don't deliver sex. I made love to you."

Of course he was right. She wanted to cower, to cry, to run, but instead she shrugged, some perverse instinct driving her on, pushing her to deny his assessment, to deny any claim he might try to make on her. He was ripping the fabric of her life into shreds, diverting her from her chosen path without the hint of a promise that he would stick around to help her create something to replace it.

She couldn't look him straight in the eye. "Like I said, semantics."

"I don't believe this." He began pacing the floor. "I really don't believe this."

He stopped directly in front of her, and the expression on his face tightened her throat in anguish at what she was doing to him, to both of them. But not enough to shame her into opening her mouth and taking back her words. The dreams and plans of a lifetime were still too strong to allow it.

"Okay, have it your way," he said after he had studied her features for several long seconds. Whatever he read there had caused him to batten down the hatches on his own emotions. That oddly vulnerable look was gone, and she couldn't tell anymore what he was thinking. Her heart ached doubly at the loss, because only minutes before they had been as close as two human beings could ever hope to be.

He finished tucking in his shirt, his movements unrushed and casual as though the fact that it was hanging loosely outside his jeans had nothing to do with the torrid sexual encounter they had just been through. "Let's just see if we can't find another tunnel out of here," he said in a quiet voice. "That way we won't have to squeeze through that opening while trying to drag a load of ingots."

"Okay, I'm game."

She straightened her spine. Well, it was back to business as usual, she thought to herself, just the way she'd always figured it would be with Deacon Baxter. She couldn't admit that it might be all her fault; she was still too busy trying to justify her wayward, ungracious behavior with everything else that had transpired. She'd always known it would come down to every man and woman for themselves, but that didn't make it any easier to bear, especially now that they had actually found something valuable enough to allow them each their dreams. She hoped to follow hers without a backward glance, just the way she knew Deke fully intended to pursue his. She suddenly realized that she didn't really know anything about his hopes and dreams except that he agreed with her about the provincialism of Justice.

"Are we taking the silver with us now?" she asked him.

His gaze connected with hers for an electric second, making her squirm inside with the reproach she could read there, but he simply answered, "No, let's leave it here. If we do find a way back to the master cave, we'll return for it, and if we don't, we'll have to come back this way, anyway. We're going to need two trips to haul it out of here as it is." A small smile tilted the corners of his mouth. "Not that I'm complaining."

"Okay." She hated the way her voice sounded so small, but she couldn't help it.

Deke hammered another eyelet into the wall and began unrolling the ever-present cord as he started off down the passage that led from the ingot room. Carly followed him, trying not to think, simply allowing the dense, otherworldly atmosphere of being closed in underground to take over her senses. Even the darkness that always hovered around the edges of their flashlight beams didn't bother her anymore. She was too numb.

She wasn't paying attention to where they were going, and when Deke suddenly stopped, she stumbled into the back of him. He automatically reached around to grab her, helping her to keep her balance, and she wanted to cry at his kindness.

"Sorry," she mumbled.

He had the right to be mad at her; if their situation had been reversed, she knew she would have been totally irate with him if he'd acted flippant and coolly uncaring after such intimacy. But of course, it was all just simple physical interaction with him, it didn't involve his emotions because he wasn't about to settle down or get serious. She was the one who had sworn she had plans for her life and who now wanted to renege in favor of love.

Her mouth went dry. There it was before she was ready for it, the *L*-word, something she had never envisioned happening to her in the middle of moldy dirt floors and claustrophobic stone walls. She had certainly never before visualized jeans and sleeping bags when she dreamed of a romantic night of love.

Still, the onyx room was beautiful, one part of her insisted with perfect logic, and certainly unique. She felt herself begin to giggle wildly, as waves of hysteria began washing up against her normally rational thought processes.

In her shock over the discovery of her feelings, she didn't realize that Deke was still stopped in front of her. "What is it?" she finally asked.

"This is definitely not the way out," he said, and his voice held an odd note that sent a shiver down her spine. When he tried to turn her back in the direction they had come she immediately resisted.

"What is it? What did you see?"

She pushed past him, shining her light along the tunnel floor ahead. When its beam picked out a very human skeleton lying directly in their path, she screamed and dropped the flashlight, turning quickly to find that Deke was waiting to shelter her in his arms. She didn't argue as she clung to him.

"I've never seen an actual human skeleton before," she said in a shaky voice. "Do you have any idea who it is?"

"I'm afraid so."

She looked up at his serious expression, then gathered her courage to glance back to where the skeleton lay stretched out across the passage. After the second shock had passed, she found it wasn't as hard as she'd thought to look at the poor man.

And male it seemed to be. The remains of some of the clothes, including a battered hat, pants and a crudely sewn leather vest, clung to the bones which were an awful yellowish-white color. As she looked closer, she could see that one hand was outstretched to clutch at a large canvas sack that lay just in front of it.

"Arvil Crook?" she whispered.

"Arvil Crook." Deke gave her a squeeze then walked over to carefully prod the sack. "Looks like he never made it to Texas, after all."

He bent down and opened the canvas to peer inside. "Well, what do you know," he said, a grin suddenly splitting his face. "More ingots."

"He must have been on his way out with them." Carly croaked, frowning. "How come he didn't make it?"

Deke flashed the beam of his light farther down the passage. Carly could see that the opening was blocked by an enormous pile of rocks that looked like the work of dynamite. Off to one side, lay a smaller pile and a pickax.

"He was trying to dig through that wall of rock," she said. "Why didn't he squeeze around the boulder like we did?"

"Probably for the same reason that entrance got sealed off. My guess is that there was an earthquake, a minor tremor while he was down here. They hit this area every now and again. Usually they don't do much damage on the surface, but this one must have caused that cave-in, closing up the tunnel he'd been using to come and go from the silver room and closing up the passage we used as well."

"Then what opened it up again? Another earthquake?"

"Probably. It explains how we managed to find that silver so easily when no one else besides Arvil ever had."

She shuddered. "He certainly had a lot of misfortune in his life. First his wife dies and then he discovers a fortune but before he can get it out, an earthquake comes along and seals him underground, silver and all.''

''Yeah. Some guys are just born unlucky.''

She ignored the sarcastic implications in his tone. ''Shouldn't we bury him or something?''

''Why? He's got a magnificent tomb all to himself, just like a Pharaoh.''

She looked unconvinced.

''What do you want me to do?''

''I think we should take him out of here and give him a proper burial. He tried so hard to get to the surface, just think how awful it was for him to realize he had the power to change his children's lives and he was never going to be able to use it.'' Her expression was softly pleading. ''Please, Deke, he deserves to have the light of day shine on his face one last time.''

''All right,'' he said, shaking his head at her whimsy but smiling nonetheless. ''I'll come back in a couple of days and haul him out of here and bury him.''

He took a step, then turned back to stare down at the remains of Arvil Crook. As Carly watched, he reached down and gently closed the canvas mouth on the bag of ingots. ''They've kept each other company this long.''

As he straightened, he pivoted on his heel then headed back down the tunnel.

''Rest in peace, Arvil,'' Carly whispered before she turned to follow him.

Now that Deke had brought up the subject of earthquakes, Carly was anxious to pack up the ingots and get the heck out from underneath the tons of rock she knew lay above their heads. She also dreaded squirming through that narrow opening again, but if that was the only way to get out of this place, then she would certainly do it.

She found she wasn't brave enough to attempt to squeeze through the crevice by herself, so she waited until Deke could help her. He went first, pulling her along behind him then returning to gather up the ingots. All in all it took him four trips to move them from the onyx room. Carly had never felt so relieved as she did when Deke emergèd from the opening for the final time.

Getting the silver down the hill outside the mouth of the cave turned out to be a quick and efficient piece of work with Deke in charge. He didn't waste a moment or a movement. It made her wonder about the work he'd done if he hadn't been climbing mountains. She had the suspicion that he'd wasted his talents terribly. He was obviously a born leader and a quick thinker as he directed her to various tasks.

It was close to eight o'clock and just about dark before all the equipment and the silver were in the camp. Neither of them said much as they set up for the night. Deke commented on the rain that had fallen while they'd been inside the cave, and Carly mentioned how much warmer it was than yesterday, all the while thinking that there was no longer any reason for shared body heat, not that they'd needed one the first time around.

Deke busied himself gathering wood while Carly washed her face and hands in the nearby stream. Then she opened the cans containing their dinner, which he handed to her after he had the fire going. He hardly even glanced at her the entire time, and he seemed to have forgotten his fascination with her underwear or anything else about her.

Carly wasn't sure whether she was relieved or disappointed. No, she quickly admitted to herself, that wasn't true. She was devastated at not being the center of his attention anymore. The loss was hard to bear, especially feeling as guilty and miserable as she did. She called herself seven different kinds of fool for cutting herself off from Deke's attention before it was absolutely necessary. The only comfort she could extract from the situation was the fact that she'd been the first one to sever the ties, before he was able to get around to it, but when she thought about the long, cool night ahead she decided her pride was misplaced and her timing was lousy.

Chapter Nine

Deke sat on his sleeping bag, staring into the fire. So much for his gallant conduct, he thought. Genghis Khan and Attila the Hun had nothing on him when it came to subtlety of expression and civilized manners. He'd never known a woman as refined and cultured as Carly, not to mention sleek, beautiful and sexy. Everything about her drove him crazy, and what did he do about it? He ravished her on a damned onyx altar like some rutting high priest conducting a fertility rite. She now had conclusive proof that he didn't know how to treat a lady, not that she'd needed it. He knew she had long ago decided that he couldn't lay claim to a single romantic bone in his body.

He glanced across the flames at her, his expression morose. Obviously she wasn't about to forgive him. She sat on top of her sleeping bag, her long legs stretched gracefully to one side, her spine naturally straight, her entire posture as slim and supple as a ballerina's.

He deliberately looked in the other direction. There was no way he could turn back the clock and handle things differently. He wasn't even sure he wanted to when his mind pictured her lying beneath him, her body as tight with arousal as his had been. A guy didn't forget moments like that, not easily, anyway. Romantic or not he wanted to take her again and again until they both became numb from the pleasure of their united bodies. Only then would he release her to become the proper Carly Riddle once again.

His gaze focused inward as he used his imagination to renegotiate every square inch of her silky skin, running metaphoric hands and eyes over the curves of her hips and breasts. It made his blood run hot, but that didn't stop him. Instead, he allowed his brain cells to take that extra step and add memories of some of the physical sensations he had experienced. It sure beat pining over what was past.

"What are you going to do with your share of the silver?" Her voice drifted to him from across the fire, as soft and feminine as the rest of her. He was still amazed that she had ended up so polished. She'd only shown a spark of her potential during her years of growing up in Justice. No one else in town spoke the way she did, so distinctly and clearly. She didn't come across as phony or forced, her soft, easy diction was just a part of the natural elegance she displayed even when crawling up the side of a hill.

When he didn't answer right away, she added, "Will Elvie's share be enough to allow him to run his farm the way he's planning?"

"It should be, if he invests it right." He picked up a twig and began toying with it.

"So, what are you going to do with your share?"

He tossed the twig into the fire, watching as the flames engulfed and consumed it, leaving only a slender piece of ash that soon crumbled into black dust. "You'll probably laugh if I tell you."

"No I won't."

She was so insistent, he might as well get it over with and spill the rest of his guts. In the small parameters of Justice she would find out soon enough, anyway. "Ever since I found out that Artie wants to sell her farm, I've been thinking about buying it."

She wasn't simply surprised, she looked as though she had swallowed one of those silver ingots whole. "You're kidding. Since when did you want to become a farmer?"

He shrugged. "Since those times when I was a kid, helping Elvie around his place. I've always loved the land, but I didn't allow myself to do anything about it. After high school, I had to get out of Justice so I could come to terms with my past and get my head screwed on straight."

He could see that she gave his answer serious consideration. She was silent for several minutes, and then she asked in a low voice, "You mean about being adopted?"

"That was part of it. I always felt like I didn't belong, even though Mom and Dad tried their darnedest to prove otherwise. I was angry at my birth mother for wanting to get rid of me. Hell, I was mad at the whole world. I thought life was being unfair to me." He chuckled mirthlessly. "And of course it was. Life is unfair to everyone in one way or another."

Her smile was slow and thoughtful. "I suppose that's true, isn't it?"

"It took coming home again to purge the anger from my soul." And you, Carly Riddle, to shed your soft light on some of the other dark aspects I had hidden there, he thought.

They sat quietly for a moment, connected by the words they had spoken and the concealing, understanding dark.

"I guess it took leaving home for me to free mine," she finally added softly.

He couldn't make out her expression because her head was slightly turned away from him, but he could see her determined profile etched against the firelight and his heart sank. He'd been hoping she would agree with him, that she would point out how she had come to exactly the same conclusion since coming home. She didn't.

"Are you going to run your farm alone? That's a lot of work for one person."

He felt a brief moment of anger that she could act so calm and unencumbered by the sticky ties and entangling emotions that were tearing him up inside. How else could she sit there and quietly inquire about such surface matters, things that any neighbor or acquaintance might ask. He hoped he could keep what he was feeling under wraps and maintain a normal tone of voice instead of succumbing to his gut instinct to grab her and shake her until she admitted that she felt the same way. If she did.

"Elvie worked his place alone, didn't he?" he finally replied.

"Yes. But Elvie doesn't need a whole lot, his lifestyle is about as simple as you can get. Somehow I don't see you living all alone like that."

"Maybe you should stay here and keep me company." He tossed the suggestion off casually, but he wasn't feeling very casual as he waited tensely for her answer. If she replied negatively this time, he would have to forget the dreams he had begun nurturing about the two of them.

"No, I couldn't possibly stay," she replied quickly. "There are people who expect me back, friends who helped me get my start."

"Yeah, that's what I figured," he answered with a bleak smile.

He'd never felt so alone in his entire life.

"Deacon Baxter buying a farm," she said, shaking her head in amazement. She looked straight across the tops of the yellow flames at him until she met his eyes. "You are just full of surprises."

He shrugged, uncomfortable with her scrutiny. "Yeah."

"What about your partner in South America?"

He paused for a moment as an image of the last time he had seen Bill filled his mind. Had he known even then that he would never be returning? He remembered feeling a sense of finality as they shook hands, but he hadn't given it a second thought at the time. "Bill will do fine without me. He's got Esteban to look after him."

"Is that the little boy you were telling me about?"

"Yeah. He's been working on worming his way into Bill's heart, and I think he's succeeded. Just before I left he had talked Bill into letting him move his few possessions into the apartment. For safekeeping." Deke chuckled to himself. "He's a pretty special kid."

"Sounds like someone else I knew in high school," she said softly.

"It's different for him than it was for me," he quickly pointed out. "Esteban knows his parents are dead. He's been forced to look out for himself since that time. Although he's only nine years old, he's doing a better job of it than many adults could, including me."

"In any case, I wish you all the best with your farm, Deke." Her voice was filled with warmth and sincerity. Why couldn't she feel as much tenderness for him as she did for his farm, he wondered sadly.

"Maybe I can show you around the place after all the legalities are taken care of and I move in."

"I'll probably be gone before that happens."

He felt her answer like a punch in the gut and silently cursed his folly. He must be a glutton for punishment, setting himself up for her rejection like that when he knew how she felt about leaving Justice. "Oh, yeah, right."

He dumped the rest of his coffee into the fire, enjoying the harsh sizzling sound it made. He felt like hurling the cup into the black void of the night, not that it would change anything. Carly was making it clear that she had plans that didn't include him, especially now that he'd told her he intended to settle down in Justice, a place she'd only returned to temporarily.

As he watched, Carly set her cup down close to the fire. She was getting ready to go to bed. He felt a surge of panic well up inside him as he realized he'd already ruined his chances for a permanent connection with her, and now his last opportunity to possess her was about to slip away, as well. He couldn't let that happen, not when he knew how quickly he could get her to respond to him and how good they were together.

No matter how opposite their outlooks on the various aspects of life, when it came to physical joining, she seemed to be as vulnerable to the process as he was. Just the memory of her moans and sighs, the feel of her soft body pressed against him, made him light-headed with desire. Surely there couldn't be any harm in trying to get close to her just one more time. It would be something to fuel his dreams after she left for Paris.

He crossed the small space between them. She was kneeling on the edge of the sleeping bag, about to slip inside and commence that damned, modest female ritual of squirming out of her clothes undercover. Her shoes, socks, blouse and sweater lay nestled in a neat pile on top of the backpack. He knelt down beside her, his hands gripping her arms and turning her so he could see her face in the dancing firelight.

"There's an easier way than getting undressed inside a sleeping bag. Let me show you."

He could see her swallow, the muscles of her throat working smoothly beneath her skin. "Are you sure that's a good idea?" she whispered in a shaky voice.

"It's the only idea I've got, so it had better be good."

He reached out to grasp the hem of her T-shirt, pulling it over her head, sliding the material down her arms. The muscles in his jaw slackened when he saw her upper body clad only in that provocative scrap of silk. Without taking his eyes from her, he tugged off his own shirt. The crackle of the fire sounded abnormally loud in his ears for a second, but then Carly reached out to touch his chest and even that receded into the background along with everything else that wasn't contained in the small space between their two bodies.

Deke grabbed her hand and kissed the back of it, then turned it over to run his tongue across the palm. She tasted sweet. She shuddered, and the skin across his shoulders tightened in response. He used her fingers to caress his face, then guided them until he could hook them into the waistband of his jeans. Without saying a word, he reached for the opening to her jeans, quickly undoing the snap and zipper, then sliding them down her legs. He pushed the material as far as it would go considering her kneeling position, then slid his hand back up along her thigh and over her hip, making sure to pull the material of her panties taut as he went across.

He was so excited he thought he might explode, but he wasn't about to relinquish this chance to bathe his senses with the sight of her clad in such scanty attire. Her body looked as beautiful as it had felt in the dark, and he knelt there paralyzed for countless seconds from the overall effect as he realized he had never really seen her like this, that parts of her had always been covered by her clothing or hidden by the dark.

He filled his hands with her breasts, squeezing them gently as he slipped his thumbs underneath the lace edges and across her nipples. She gasped and he did it again. Her breasts were rounder, fuller, than they appeared beneath her clothes.

He traced the line of her body, past her hips and down along her thighs. No marble statue could match the graceful contours he felt there, the smooth sculpted beauty. Her legs were long and slim, ideal for wrapping around a man and sending him over the edge, he thought, moaning as his lower body hardened beyond anything he'd ever experienced, aware that the distinction between pain and pleasure had narrowed another notch.

He'd barely begun to explore the heights of where this passion could take them. She was in for one hell of a ride. He intended to make sure they were both flung out into the void, totally dependent on each other for breath itself until they consumed everything that was in them to give.

He tried to restrain his instincts, but he was growing impatient now. He released her for the brief seconds it took him to unzip the sleeping bag and spread it open on the ground.

He quickly pushed her onto the flannel, following her down and reaching along her legs to yank her jeans off. He was careering wildly out of control, his brain sending him conflicting signals until he thought he would go crazy in the next split second. He wanted her naked with her legs around him, and yet he wanted to drink in the sight of her in her classy underthings, a vision that belonged to this night and to him alone. Now, however, was not the time for cool and slow. Considering the state he was in he decided to opt for naked.

Obviously Carly had the same general idea in mind because she was fumbling with the metal button on his jeans. He couldn't stay still long enough to let her succeed on her own but pushed her hands aside and quickly wrenched the pants open, removing them with an efficiency of motion that was admirable in a man who was basically lost to rational decision-making. He'd better slow down a little, he told himself, otherwise he was going to peak before he could take Carly along with him.

He lay beside her, his eyes scanning her body in the soft firelight, his hands clenching into fists as he kept them off her for a moment while he tried to cool down so he could function like a human being and not an animal. Remember the cave, the last sane part of his brain reminded him. Remember you promised yourself to give her refined and romantic lovemaking.

He squeezed his eyes shut tight. Hell, he would give her anything if she would only put him out of his misery.

"What's the matter, Deke," her soft voice interrupted his agonizing thoughts.

"I'm trying to calm down, to make this the way I know you want it." He opened his eyes to gauge her reaction.

She met his gaze directly. "And how is that?"

"Civilized. Romantic. I'm sorry I can't remember the French words you told me, but the sight of you is driving everything clear out of my head, including the sense I was born with."

"No matter," she told him with a straight face, but he could see the pleased little smile tugging at the corners of her mouth. "Sense isn't high on the list of what I need from you right now." She moved closer to him, leaning over his face until her hair tickled his nose and he could smell its clean, flowery scent. "Shall I take my underwear off so it doesn't distract you anymore? Which piece shall I remove first?"

"Carly." Her name came out in a croaky whisper; it was all he could manage. He was lucky he was still breathing.

She pushed him over until he was on his back. He could feel his chest rising and falling in ragged motions as his lungs labored for air. He wasn't sure what she intended to do; all he knew was that he was malleable clay in her hands.

He watched as she raised herself on one elbow then hooked her free hand inside the lacy border of the panties and worked them down her legs and off into her hand. She held them up for a moment, before tossing them aside. Deke knew he was about to discover if a man's body could withstand this kind of torment and survive to tell the tale.

He reached up to pull her on top of him, sliding her down onto that part of him that had suffered the longest. "Be gentle with me, sweetheart," he murmured, his hands framing her face. He tugged urgently until her mouth came down to meld with his, at the same time lifting his body to fuse them together in every possible way. It was the last coherent action he was to remember for a long, long time.

FOR THE SECOND TIME in her life, Carly awoke inside a sleeping bag next to a warm, male body. This was getting to be a regular habit and one that she knew she could grow very accustomed to, especially if she omitted the sleeping bag and concentrated on the warm male body. She snuggled against Deke, enjoying the feel of his arm around her waist, holding her close. She knew without even seeing his face that he was awake; she could feel the force of his awareness all around her. She wondered what he was thinking, then quickly decided that she didn't really want to know. It was enough that they were here together one more time.

She looked back over her shoulder at him. "Hi," she said softly.

"Good morning."

His gaze softened for a moment before settling into an expression that seemed almost artificial after the intimacy they had again shared. Obviously he had come to some sort of decision within himself about how to act with her this morning. The openness he had displayed last night was gone, and in its place was a veneer of friendliness and warmth and just a touch of sincere regret. It was as though a mask had descended to cover the man she had been learning to know and love. This man was a stranger, and her heart cried at the loss.

She wanted to sob hysterically and cling to him, but she still had some pride left. She'd worked too hard and too long to give up her career on the chance that Deke wanted a permanent relationship. In her mind it was better to end it now rather than later when it would only be more difficult. Deke had the right idea. She resolutely decided that she could play the game as well as he could and she would, no matter what it cost her.

"I guess we'd better get a move on, huh?" she asked with cheerful bravado. "I can't wait to tell Uncle Elvie the news."

"He's going to be surprised, all right."

"I was thinking maybe I could pay Mrs. Harbaugh to come and stay with him. She's certainly reliable, and she's always looking for ways to supplement that pension from the railroad that her husband left her. That way I won't have to wait for my mother to get back to get him settled on the farm, and I'll be able to pack my things and get on with my life.''

He nodded, unsmiling. "Good idea."

Well, that answered her question about how he would react when she talked about leaving, she thought sadly. She watched him slide out of the sleeping bag, then turned away when he stood up. It seemed too personal now to view his nakedness. She felt as if she no longer had the right to possess his body, even with her eyes.

He seemed to have some of the same feelings, because he never even turned around to look at her when she sat up and reached for her things, dressing herself while she sat half in and half out of the sleeping bag. He didn't even pay attention while she rustled inside her backpack for clean underwear, didn't notice that the slinky little pair she pulled out had blue lace up the sides and a matching bra that hooked in the front.

She took a deep breath and swallowed hard to keep herself from crying. She would not cry in front of him or allow him to see that any of this affected her in any way. Sheer will and pride were the only things she had to see her through, and she intended to use them both to hold herself together.

It was over. His agreement with her assessment couldn't have been more clear. Her mouth turned down at the corners, and her throat tightened painfully. She would never see him the way she had last night, never again have the chance to be wild and wanton and out of control in his arms. She doubted anyone could top Deke in that department.

She grabbed a long-sleeved shirt from the pack and stuffed the rest of the things she wouldn't be needing inside, snapping it closed. He was more man than she had ever dreamed of handling. She'd thought she had included everything in her plans for her future; she had even prided herself on creating a bigger and better life for herself than many of the other girls in her high school class, who had simply wanted to settle down with their Justice boyfriends and get married.

Something inside her stubbornly refused to deviate from the path she had started out on, the one that included life as she knew it in Paris, even if it was at the expense of what she had discovered right here at home. She certainly hadn't counted on falling in love with a Justice boy herself, had never even believed she was susceptible to the breed. Deke had his life to live and she had hers.

She watched him fashion a sledlike contraption out of canvas so Zerelda could drag the ingots along behind her until they got to the car. Carly ended up with a larger share of the original equipment, but she gladly shouldered the burden. For one thing, she was certainly more fit than she'd been on the trip out here, and anyway, the heavier load helped keep her mind from wandering onto trails where it no longer had any business going. Whenever she found her thoughts heading in a fruitless direction, she would quicken her steps and yank at the strap around her waist that helped hold the pack. Her legs would protest the added strain, but she would ignore the burning in her muscles until she could stand it no more and then she would relent. The relief was so great, it filled her mind for several blessed minutes until she started the cycle all over again.

Deke was pleasant, even appearing nonchalant, although occasionally Carly thought she could detect tenseness behind the casual facade. But no, that had to be her willful imagination at work, trying to persuade her she should throw herself into his arms and let the chips fall where they may. She knew it was impossible, even though her stubborn mind kept hammering at unworkable solutions. Deke wanted to stay in Justice. She had her work in Paris. He wanted to farm, which meant he was tied to the land forever. She wanted to travel around Europe in her spare time.

She had to face up to reality. They had come together because fate had decided to play a trick on her. Everyone knew the fulfillment of dreams always came at a price.

Deke was giving her an easy way out by signaling his intentions this way; he was allowing her to save face. Instead of being a fool and pushing things to the limit, she had to let go now. Hard as it was, she had to mentally wean each finger away from its desire to clutch at Deke so they could both get on with their lives. How could Paris and the continuation of the career she had fought so hard to attain not heal her broken heart?

DEKE RODE THE HORSE back to the house, and because he was able to travel as the crow flies, he beat Carly, who was driving the car. When she pulled up she could see that Elvie was jubilant at the news. She hoped it was all right that he was dancing a jig up and down her mother's porch because she certainly didn't

have the heart to interrupt his whooping and holler-
ing.

"Now, Elvie," Deke finally said in a calming voice
after Elvie's last rebel yell. He led his old friend to the
glider and sat down opposite him. "Let me tell you
how we solved this thing. We had a little help from an
unexpected direction." He proceeded to explain about
Artie and the letters and how they had also discovered a trunk full of photos, editing out the part about
her cutting the cord.

Elvie wasn't impressed. "Those were my dad-
blasted letters in the first place," he exploded, "and
if she hadn't had them we could have solved the puz-
zle even faster."

"What, a week isn't fast enough for finding the
fortune of a lifetime, old buddy?" Deke said with an
amused glance in Carly's direction. Carly felt the intimacy of that look as her heart turned over in an acute
combination of happiness and pain.

"She gave them to us very willingly, Uncle Elvie,"
she added softly.

Her uncle pulled a long-suffering look. "I suppose," he relented grudgingly.

"Now, listen, mister," Deke shook a finger at him
in mock severity. "I'm thinking of buying her farm
and settling my butt down in these parts. With your
permission I was hoping to use those photos to close
the deal." He leaned closer and dropped his voice to a
whisper. "That crafty Artie Brown will want me to
keep her museum on Jesse James going, and I figure
with all those pictures, the state might step in and take
over, thereby getting me off the hook."

Elvie, who seemed to like the idea of pulling something over on his old nemesis, readily agreed. "Sure, Deke. The photos are yours. I don't need 'em, anyway." He slapped his thigh. "Can you imagine that, Deke Baxter right here in Justice!"

Deke grinned. "We'll be neighbors, heaven help me. And if you need anything, anything at all, you'd better give me a holler."

"I will." Elvie beamed. "And you can bet the farm on it."

CARLY COULDN'T BELIEVE how the time dragged after Deke left that evening. Everything bright and shining had gone out like a light in her life, but she stalwartly assured herself that it was to be expected after the adventure she had just been on. She needed to get on with her life, get back to Paris and her friends and everything that was familiar to her. Justice wasn't her home anymore, and she shouldn't think for a minute that she was doing anything other than visiting.

Deke took care of everything, although he always managed to stop by to see Elvie whenever she wasn't home. He'd had the silver appraised, and he helped counsel Elvie on how to invest the money so that he would have a steady and comfortable income for the rest of his life. He did the same for Carly. She finally decided to relay her thanks through her uncle because she never saw Deke, and that's when she found out he must have given Elvie an edited version of what had gone on between them.

"I'm sorry things didn't work out between you and Deke, honey," he said to her one afternoon after she had broached the subject.

"There was nothing to work out, Uncle Elvie," she replied, and she tried fervently to believe it was the truth.

Elvie didn't let any grass grow under his feet, but moved out to his farm as soon as he was able to locate Mrs. Harbaugh, hire a hand and get his doctor's approval. In fact, the doctor had been astonished at the improvement of his patient and pronounced him fit enough to revert to a yearly checkup schedule. Elvie had been busy behind the scenes even before that, because he had somehow gotten connected up with the agricultural department of the university, making an agreement with them for the use of part of his land for their experimental projects. In exchange for that privilege, the university had agreed to provide students to help him farm his fields, even going so far as to give him the title of agricultural adviser.

Carly knew her uncle didn't need her help anymore. She didn't want to hang around Justice, even to await Sarah Riddle's return, so she booked her passage to France, promising her mother that she would be back for Thanksgiving. She could certainly afford the airfare. A few days before her flight, she opened an account in both her and her mother's names so her mother could draw on it as needed to supplement her schoolteaching income, assuring her a worry-free existence from now on.

Everyone's life seemed perfect, and hers would be, too, as soon as she found a job and got back into the mainstream of life as she had always yearned to live it.

She stopped to see her uncle the day before her flight was scheduled to leave. The old man looked fit and healthy, and John Alsdorf seemed to be working out fine as his foreman. She sat on the porch sipping freshly made iced tea provided by Mrs. Harbaugh as her uncle happily rambled on about what he was doing.

"You know Deke signed the papers today. He's now the official owner of the Wilkey place, lock, stock and barrel. He's even working on the state to get them to take over that confounded museum. He says he's gonna have them put a plaque up on the wall explaining how I donated those photos from my private collection and says I can even get a tax break because of it!"

"That's wonderful, Uncle Elvie," Carly said, trying to inject enough enthusiasm into her voice so he wouldn't be suspicious. The bottom line was that she truly felt excited for her uncle and happy for Deke, who seemed to be thriving in his new life. It was only she who needed to shake off this lethargy.

"He said to tell you that Zee was part of the bargain and that he's fattening her up nicely."

"Terrific."

She didn't want to hear about Deke, and yet she found herself eager to take in every little detail of what he was doing. She was proud of the way he had turned his life around, that he was doing something meaningful. He had a purpose, a direction, and she was glad of it. The Prodigal Son of Justice had turned out better than anyone had ever expected.

Chapter Ten

That evening Carly stood in front of the suitcase laid out on the bed and wondered if the shattered pieces of her heart could ever be spliced back into some semblance of normality. Unlike her love life, everything about her trip back to Paris was going smoothly. But it wasn't enough. She had hoped her head would be stuffed with all the wonderful plans and dreams that had always been her guiding light before, but it hadn't worked out that way and she found herself more unhappy than she had ever thought a human being could be.

There was no denying that she was in love with Deke; every fiber of her body ached with awareness of her feelings, and her desire for his presence was almost beyond bearing. It was as though she had absorbed his essence and combined it with her own until she was no longer the same person she had been only a month ago.

She wanted to travel and see the world. Well, now she was about to do it. She knew once she got back to Paris it would be easy to slip away on weekends to cities like Marseilles and Nice as well as other countries like Belgium and the Netherlands. Her dreams were going according to plan; the only problem was that it was at the expense of her heart.

Still, Deke had never said he wanted her permanently. She might as well just get on with it. She would still be brokenhearted, whether in Justice or Paris, she assured herself as she folded the slinky black dress she had bought last year in a small boutique in Paris. As she stared at it draped over her hands an idea popped into her mind. She knew it must have been brewing there for quite a while since it was a full-blown plan with all the details filled in. Did she dare do it? She bit her lip as the more pertinent question filled her thoughts—did she dare leave the United States for who knew how long without doing it?

She blew out a breath as she sat down beside her suitcase, the dress still in her hands. She hadn't been herself since that day when she had stood on her mother's front porch almost two months ago, watching Deacon Baxter swing his long, jean-clad legs over the leather seat of his motorcycle. Just the thought of that innocent beginning tightened her throat as waves of bittersweet nostalgia washed along her nerve endings followed by a sharp, stabbing pain in her heart. As if that weren't enough, she had to cope with a conflicting sense of thankfulness that she'd been allowed to have the experience in the first place. She must really be losing it to feel that way, but the fact remained that she did.

If she retained any claim at all to sanity, she would have to admit that flinging herself into the arms of a man who might not even open them to her was madness. She hadn't wandered onto the set of *Love Story*, for heaven's sake; she wasn't Jennifer Cavilleri forced to choose between studying music in Paris or marrying Oliver Barrett IV. Carly sighed as she remembered watching the video and sobbing into the wads of tissues she held crumpled in her hand. Was love the most important human achievement, the way the movie had insisted? She was beginning to think so, especially when in the threat of its absence nothing else felt worthwhile.

She knew she had to at least try, before she got cold feet. If things went according to the plan her mind had concocted, she wouldn't have to blurt right out that she loved him.

Two minutes later she found herself dialing Elvie's number.

"Carly, where are you? Are you in Paris yet?" Carly could tell that he was shouting. As he had once explained to her, it was necessary to yell into a telephone in proportion to the distance away the person was.

"I'm right here in Justice," she told him, repressing the urge to shout back at him. "I need to ask Deke something before I go and I don't have his phone number."

He gave it to her without a murmur before he launched excitedly into what he'd been doing. "Wait till you see my fields. Got myself a bumper crop of soybeans this year. Those kids from that fancy agriculture school actually seem to know what they're doing. I've even got a couple of acres of experimental corn planted. It's not supposed to have all that husk, can you believe that?"

"That's wonderful."

"Deke said that one portfolio of stocks we invested in has split. Smart boy, our Deke. He's always asking after you."

"That's nice," Carly replied quietly.

"He'll be glad to hear from you." With that the old man hung up abruptly, the way he always did, without saying goodbye. He figured if he was finished with the conversation, everyone else must be.

Carly stood in the hallway, biting her lip and wondering if she had the courage to face Deke before she left. Her scheme had its advantages. She could confront him with her feelings and find out his response, and if it wasn't to her liking she could leave Justice tomorrow afternoon with no one the wiser.

The element of surprise would also work to her advantage because he wouldn't have time to fabricate a reaction; it would be an honest one. Of course, she would have to be tough enough to be able to handle whatever he said or did, but she knew she would feel even more of a fool if she didn't follow through.

She had to go through with it. Dear God, she loved him, and she had to know if his finding that out would make a difference.

THE NEXT MORNING she stopped her mother's car in front of the rundown house where she had first seen Artressa Brown Wilkey. Deke had pulled away the messy vines and brambles that were threatening to engulf the little house, and he had cleaned up the yard somehow so that it looked much neater.

She reached over to her satchel, which lay on the passenger seat next to her, and pulled out the small, gift-wrapped package again, staring at it while her heart began beating like a kettledrum. This had to be the tenth time she had looked at it this morning, but she hoped if she went through this step often enough—pulling out the present and contemplating handing it to the man she loved—the terror would gradually abate. It was called aversion therapy, but so far she had only succeeded in giving herself such heart palpitations that she'd been tempted to raid the small bottle of brandy her mother kept in the cupboard.

She fingered the little box, toying with the blue ribbon that matched the masculine swirls of the wrapping paper she'd chosen. She had her plan down cold. If Deke laughed and took it as a gag, she would be forced to do so, too, even though her heart would be breaking. But if he realized the intention behind the gift, he would immediately understand what she was trying to say to him. She hadn't the least idea what would happen after that, but she figured if he still wanted her, even a little bit, she could manage the rest of it.

Deke was expecting her, but that only made her feel more nervous. She hadn't had a moment's relief since she'd had that brief telephone conversation with him last night, asking him if she could stop by before she left for Paris. He'd been somewhat terse in his reply, so she wasn't sure whether he approved of the idea or not. Her mind didn't bother to make any distinctions but was set on torturing her, and nothing she had done last night was able to knock it from the willful, one-track groove it had carved in her brain, leaving her sleepless and tired this morning.

Taking a deep breath, she gathered up her satchel and got out of the car.

DEKE TOSSED DOWN the screwdriver he'd been using to tighten the hinge on the kitchen cabinet. The place wasn't a palace yet, but it was beginning to shape up with all the attention he'd been lavishing on it. Keeping himself busy had served two purposes, and getting the house into livable shape was the lesser of them.

He sighed as he closed his toolbox. Carly was coming over to say goodbye, but he wasn't sure if it might not be better for her to just leave without subjecting him to more torment. He was getting his life in order the best way he knew how. He had a purpose and a direction, and those things would help him get through this visit today and all the days that would follow.

No one knew better than he did that he was a different person than he'd been only months ago. He knew he was light-years removed from the man who had lived his crazy life in South America. Back then he'd taken each day as it came, without a plan and without any particular direction. Why not? His body was young and strong, invincible, even. Every muscle and sinew was primed for action. Everything had changed after that night he had gotten knocked on the head; before the ache had even subsided he'd been handed that fateful letter from Elvie. Once back in Justice, he had fallen for Carly, which had changed his life and his priorities forever. Just thinking about the contrast, before and after Santa Rosaria, made his chest tighten and his throat close with emotion.

Even now he could reexperience the pain he had felt when he'd learned that she was going through with her plans, that she had made reservations to board the plane to Paris so she could fly coolly out of his life toward her dream. Damn, he didn't begrudge her a career, but she could have at least tried to fit him in. She'd never even asked.

He figured she must be pretty happy about leaving Justice. He quickly shook his head, driving away images that were too painful to contemplate. She was doing what she wanted and so was he and never the twain would meet after today. He had his farm to think about now, and he thanked all his lucky stars that this was so. Buying Artressa Wilkey's place was about to save him from himself. He'd be too busy to worry about a woman who didn't want him.

He thought he heard a noise, so he walked over to the window to peer out. Sure enough, there was Carly, heading toward his front door, but what in the name of the Sapa Inca was she wearing? He closed his eyes in pain, but couldn't help opening them to have another look. Was he going crazy, perhaps dreaming with his eyes open? He stared at the vision, but it didn't go away.

Instead, as she got closer, he could see that she was wearing one of those little black dresses that should have been outlawed years ago. It was short and clung to every curve, making his mouth water and his hands itch to touch her. He had never seen stockings as sheer as the pair she had on; they looked as though they had been woven by elves. He could tell even from here that if he touched them, they would be hopelessly snagged on the rough calluses of his hands.

He dropped the musty curtain back into place and went to the front door. As she came up the porch steps she looked up and met his eyes directly. No, he wasn't dreaming. He was surprised to note that she seemed nervous and uncomfortable. And no wonder, she probably hadn't expected to find him hanging on to the front doorknob as though he'd been waiting for her to arrive.

Her legs looked gorgeous. Of course, he'd seen them before but not coming out from beneath the short length of material that formed the skirt of her dress. No wonder she wore those silky, skimpy underthings; there wasn't enough room between her and that dress for much more than than. His heart began beating harder.

"So, you leave for Paris this afternoon," he said when she came to a halt on the other side of the screen door. He didn't mean it to sound accusing, but somehow it came out that way.

She smiled politely. "Um, yes, I am."

"Come on in." He stepped back so she could enter. "It's not much, but then we both know that Artressa wasn't much of a housekeeper."

Carly's smile widened. "No, not if her museum was anything to go by."

She stepped through the doorway, standing awkwardly by the front door, almost as though she wanted to bolt back out of it. Well, she was here now and it was so good to be able to look at her again, Deke decided he had to insure she would stay for a while at least. "Come on into the living room."

She followed him there, clutching her bag as though robbers were trying to snatch it away from her. He wondered what she had in it, but then who knew what women carried around with them. She'd carried only her backpack while they'd been looking for Jesse's stash, but that had been extenuating circumstances.

Still, she looked strange enough that he finally asked her, "Is something wrong?"

"No. That is . . . no, nothing's wrong."

"Here, why don't you put that bag down?" She set it down next to her on the floor, even though she was still standing warily just inside the door of his living room. "So how have you been?" he asked her.

"Fine."

"I guess you're packed and ready to leave home." He could have bitten his tongue at calling Justice her home, but she didn't seem offended.

She nodded. "Yes, pretty much."

"Here, sit down."

He reached over to move some magazines out of her way, disgusted with himself. What was he doing having this banal conversation with the woman he loved when he was about to lose her forever? It was crazy, insane. He watched her sit down across from him, intrigued by the graceful way she maneuvered the short skirt so her legs were covered. Or at least somewhat covered. There was still a considerable portion available for his viewing, and they ended in black high heels that managed to look dainty and dangerous at the same time. How did women get away with wearing stuff that was designed to send a guy completely over the edge?

"It looks like you've really settled in here," she commented.

"Yeah, as best as I can under the circumstances. I'm going to build another house. This one leaves a lot to be desired as a residence."

"That's great, Deke." She smiled. "I don't know how Artie lived here for as long as she did."

Even his name on her tongue made him shiver with desire and longing and pain. He wished he could remain cool and aloof from the situation, but he found that his impulse to blurt out something more to the point than "how are you" was growing stronger every second. He didn't think he could take much more of this.

Neither of them said anything for the next few minutes. Carly was staring at that awful landscape painting that hung on the wall as though her life depended on it. He hadn't taken the damn thing down because he didn't want to expose the lighter-colored wallpaper behind it. She probably felt she had to make conversation, and she had already run out of things to say. Why had she come here if she felt so awkward about seeing him again? Hell, he guessed it was up to him to throw another dead-end conversational gem out into the ring. He struggled with himself for a moment before forcing his tongue to action.

"So, when do you leave?"

"About three o'clock."

"It's nice of you to come say goodbye." He couldn't believe he was making such an idiotic statement when it was the farthest thing from the truth he'd ever uttered.

"I had to come. I forgot to do something."

"Oh." He hesitated a moment then asked bluntly. "What?"

She didn't answer.

What the hell is going on, he wondered as Carly continued to stare straight ahead. What the hell was she doing here if she didn't even want to talk to him? Well, fine. If she wanted him to sit here like a rock, he could do that as easily as the next guy. A hint of her perfume whiffed past him just then, and it brought in its wake such a flood of memories, feelings and emotions, he was barely able to keep from groaning. He clamped his teeth together and smiled grimly.

"Deke... I have something for you, kind of a going-away present." She reached down to pull a gaily wrapped package from her bag, holding it out to him. It was small and flat. "I... here."

She handed it to him, and he automatically shifted across the small space between them so he could take it, although he wasn't able to hide the expression of astonishment on his face. She never wanted to see him again and yet she had brought him a going-away present? He was definitely losing what was left of his sanity.

"Go ahead, open it." She cleared her throat. "I want to know what you think."

He ripped the ribbon and paper away, then lifted the lid. Now he knew he had wandered into the ozone. He looked down into the box to see a pair of men's briefs. Brief was certainly the word to describe them. They weren't as skimpy as Carly's had been, but not by a whole lot. He started to lift them out of the box.

He stared at her, speechless, as dawning comprehension began to fill him. Could she really be saying what he thought she was saying? He looked directly into her eyes, his own blazing with an intense combination of hope and fear.

"Carly..."

"I thought you might return the favor and model them for me. That is, if you want to."

He gripped the box in his hands, crushing the sides until they were flattened. "Hell, yes, I want to. You must know by now that I'm not the type who favors fancy underwear for men, but if it will keep you around, even just for the rest of the summer, I'll model them on Main Street."

"The truth is I don't care about the underwear. It was just the means to an end. If you want to skip it and take the direct route, I won't object."

He tossed the box aside and reached for her, pulling her into his lap. She came easily into his embrace, where he held her tight and close, smelling the fragrance of her hair, feeling the slim contours of her body that he knew fit so perfectly against his. "Carly, I have to tell you something. Maybe I should have said it before, but I was too scared to admit the way I really felt, and I . . ."

"I love you, Deke," she interrupted him to say softly. "I love you more than being in Paris."

He grasped the back of her neck in his hand so he could look deeply into her eyes. "Thank God," he said, and he could feel the kilowatt power of his happiness blazing in his smile. "I love you more than anything anywhere on this earth." He kissed her softly, and he could feel the answering smile on her lips. "Or below it, for that matter."

His mouth covered hers with more purpose this time, and he rocked his lips against hers, slanting them until the contact he craved was achieved. He kissed her for minutes, hours, a lifetime passed in that one kiss, and then he pulled back so he could see her beautiful hazel eyes.

"Does that excuse for jockey shorts have a matching feminine version, you know, like his and hers?" he asked solemnly.

Her grin was wide and wicked. "I'm wearing them."

Carly couldn't stop smiling as she returned Deke's gaze. She knew she looked like an idiot, but she didn't care. What else could you do when the man you loved with utter and total abandon told you that he loved you, too. Thank you, Uncle Elvie. Thank you, Jesse James.

"So. What happens now?" Deke asked solemnly.

"I . . . I guess that depends on you."

His eyes flared with an emotion so strong she was sure it could cut through steel like a laser beam. It brought tears to hers. "I would say that it depends on whether you could be happy living in Missouri with only occasional visits to Paris."

She realized her hands were clenched and consciously relaxed them. His gaze never left her face. "I'd be happy to spend the rest of my life in a sleeping bag if you were in it, too."

He started forward to kiss her again, then stopped himself just inches away from her. "What happened to that sophisticated Frenchman you thought was such a good match?"

She shrugged. "He turned into a natural Missouri man with a twang."

Deke set her on her feet then jumped up from his chair, scooping her up and twirling her around and around before setting her on the floor, where he kissed her with rough abandon.

"Come with me," he said gruffly. "I want to show you the rest of the house."

He led her through the living room and up the narrow staircase to his bedroom. He hadn't done anything with the upstairs except buy a bed and a set of sheets, but it was functional enough for his purpose now. She held on tightly to his hand, as though she would never let him go. Which was a good thing, he thought, because he wasn't going to release her, not ever again.

Carly went more than willingly when he tugged her down onto the bed. When he looked at her and smiled, her heart turned over with joy at his love-filled expression. It was a good thing her capacity for happiness was infinite. She couldn't wait for them to begin their new life together.

Epilogue

Six months later, Carly sat in the spare room she had set up as her office. She looked around with satisfaction at the fax machine and computer, still unable to believe that she had pulled it off. Then again, she thought proudly, why not? She had a master's degree in business, and so she was eminently qualified to start a mail-order company featuring Parisian fashions. She was beginning small, with accessories that could be shipped easily, but she hoped her concept would put her a step ahead of the rest. She planned to explain all the finer nuances of Frenchwomen's dressing with photographs and illustrations, showing how her accessories could help American women achieve that subtle, continental flair.

As she was daydreaming about her ultimate jump into the full ensemble of women's clothing, Deke appeared in the doorway dressed in jeans and a flannel shirt with the sleeves rolled partway up his strong forearms. He looked good enough to eat.

"What are you doing back so soon? I thought you were going to start planting the winter groundcover." She felt pleased to be familiar with some of the terminology of farming, although it still amazed her to be spouting off such things.

"I decided it could wait until tomorrow, Mrs. Baxter. The weather's supposed to be better then, anyway."

She smiled. "I still can't believe French Chic is on its way."

"I knew you would figure out a way to bring culture to the Midwest. When I saw you on your mother's porch I said to myself, this woman has a head for business."

"You said no such thing." She chuckled. "And anyway, I'd better have a head for business after spending all that time getting educated about it." She swiveled her chair around so she could face him more fully as she said in an excited voice, "We're almost ready to roll with the catalog. Georges is doing the artwork in his studio on the Rue Marbeuf."

"I love it when you speak French."

She smiled at him teasingly. "Oh, really?"

"Yes, really. Come here and talk French to me." He squatted down next to her chair, sliding his hands around her waist.

"I'm working, Deke," she said, squirming in his grip but only a little. "Listen to this catalog copy and tell me what you think. 'Frenchwomen always remain faithful to their fragrance, using one perfume as their personal signature, so that they are always associated with it and remembered by it.'"

"I remember you by it." He nuzzled her neck, then licked her skin. "But that's because you taste like French sin, *guapa*."

She sighed happily. "I like it when you call me *guapa*."

"Do you know why you like it?"

"Sure," she said, raising her arms to encircle his neck. "It's because I'm a sucker for foreign endearments."

"Wrong." His hands were wandering up the sides of her rib cage and his smile grew wicked. "It's because when I say it, it's usually the prelude to what most farmers like to euphemistically call a roll in the hay." He pulled one hand free so he could hold it up to forestall her protest, although she didn't make one. "But then again, I'm not most farmers."

She giggled, watching him as he reached into his back pocket and pulled out his wallet. "What are you doing?" she asked, suddenly impatient for his full attention. She had discovered that one of the benefits of being married to a farmer was that he could take an extended break when the occasion or the need demanded.

He grinned as he extracted a paper from underneath the clear plastic where his license was located and unfolded it. "Now, where was I? Ah yes, we were discussing a roll in the hay, weren't we. But what I actually wanted to say was *'J'ai envie de t'embrasser partout.'*"

"Deke!" Her cheeks immediately flushed with pleasure and the blood started pounding in her veins. "Where did you learn that?"

"From one of your books." He scooped her out of her chair and carried her from her office into the master bedroom next door. "I've been practicing saying it all day."

"Do you know what it means?" she whispered.

"Sure do." He dropped her lightly onto the multi-hued comforter and proceeded to lie down beside her, his hand immediately going to the soft material of her turtleneck as he pulled it free of her jeans. "It means, 'I want to kiss you all over,' and I do. I'm also planning to demonstrate the rest of my in-depth knowledge of a woman's psyche, so watch closely."

Carly sighed with deep pleasure as she gave herself up to him. A roll in the hay, indeed. She almost giggled, but Deke's hands caressing her body wouldn't allow anything other than a soft, heartfelt moan of surrender.

He had been right all along, of course. Semantics had nothing to do with it. She didn't care what the sharing of their bodies was called as long as she got to experience it as often as possible. When a woman was in love she didn't have to have special words or fancy packaging and she didn't want some kind of sophisticated mind game going on beneath the surface of the physical reality. She simply needed her man to love her without reservation, holding nothing back in the quest to become one flesh.

"I love you, Deke," she whispered, looking straight into his eyes. They blazed back at her with enough love to last a lifetime.

"And I love you."

It had all started with the search to find an outlaw's hidden stash. But what it had turned into was a permanent date with her very own outlaw.

Calloway Corners

In September, Harlequin is proud to bring readers four involving, romantic stories about the Calloway sisters, set in Calloway Corners, Louisiana. Written by four of Harlequin's most popular and award-winning authors, you'll be enchanted by these sisters and the men they love!

MARIAH by Sandra Canfield
JO by Tracy Hughes
TESS by Katherine Burton
EDEN by Penny Richards

As an added bonus, you can enter a sweepstakes contest to win a trip to Calloway Corners, and meet all four authors. Watch for details in all Calloway Corners books in September.

CAL93

Take 4 bestselling love stories FREE

Plus get a FREE surprise gift!

Special Limited-time Offer

Mail to Harlequin Reader Service®

3010 Walden Avenue
P.O. Box 1867
Buffalo, N.Y. 14269-1867

YES! Please send me 4 free Harlequin American Romance® novels and my free surprise gift. Then send me 4 brand-new novels every month, which I will receive months before they appear in bookstores. Bill me at the low price of $2.71 each plus 25¢ delivery and applicable sales tax, if any.*That's the complete price and—compared to the cover prices of $3.50 each—quite a bargain! I understand that accepting the books and gift places me under no obligation ever to buy any books. I can always return a shipment and cancel at any time. Even if I never buy another book from Harlequin, the 4 free books and the surprise gift are mine to keep forever.

154 BPA AJJF

Name	(PLEASE PRINT)	
Address	Apt. No.	
City	State	Zip

This offer is limited to one order per household and not valid to present Harlequin American Romance® subscribers. *Terms and prices are subject to change without notice. Sales tax applicable in N.Y.

UAM-93R

©1990 Harlequin Enterprises Limited

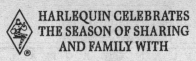

THANKS

AMERICAN ROMANCE INVITES YOU TO CELEBRATE A DECADE OF SUCCESS....

It's a year of celebration for American Romance, as we commemorate a milestone achievement—ten years of bringing you the kinds of romance novels you want to read, by the authors you've come to love.

And to help celebrate, Harlequin American Romance has a gift for you! A limited hardcover collection of two of Harlequin American Romance's most popular earlier titles, written by two of your favorite authors:

ANNE STUART—*Partners in Crime*
BARBARA BRETTON—*Playing for Time*

This unique collection will not be available in retail stores and is only available through this exclusive offer.

Send your name, address, zip or postal code, along with six original proof-of-purchase coupons from any Harlequin American Romance novel published in August, September or October 1993, plus $3.00 for postage and handling (check or money order—please do not send cash), payable to Harlequin Books, to:

In the U.S.
American Romance 10th Anniversary
Harlequin Books
P.O. Box 9057
Buffalo, NY 14269-9057

In Canada
American Romance 10th Anniversary
Harlequin Books
P.O. Box 622
Fort Erie, Ontario
L2A 5X3

(Please allow 4-6 weeks for delivery. Hurry! Quantities are limited. Offer expires November 30, 1993.)

HARLEQUIN AMERICAN ROMANCE
10TH ANNIVERSARY
ONE PROOF-OF-PURCHASE   092-KBA